NOT A CLUE

NOT A CLUE

A FORSYTH AND HAY MYSTERY

CLUE

JANET BRONS

TouchWood
Editions

TouchWood Editions
touchwoodeditions.com

LIBRARY AND ARCHIVES CANADA CATALOGUING IN PUBLICATION
Brons, Janet, 1954–, author
Not a clue / Janet Brons.

(A Forsyth and Hay mystery)
Issued in print and electronic formats.
ISBN 978-1-77151-147-6 (paperback)

I. Title. II. Series: Brons, Janet, 1954– . Forsyth and Hay mystery.

PS8603.R653N68 2015   C813'.6   C2015-904113-9

Editor: Frances Thorsen
Design: Pete Kohut
Cover image: Vladone, istockphoto.com

 Canadian Heritage / Patrimoine canadien Canada Council for the Arts / Conseil des Arts du Canada BRITISH COLUMBIA ARTS COUNCIL

We gratefully acknowledge the financial support for our publishing activities
from the Government of Canada through the Canada Book Fund and the Canada
Council for the Arts, and from the Province of British Columbia through the
British Columbia Arts Council and the Book Publishing Tax Credit.

The interior pages of this book have been printed on 100% post-consumer
recycled paper, processed chlorine free, and printed with vegetable-based inks.

1 2 3 4 5   19 18 17 16 15

PRINTED IN CANADA

To Chantal

ONE

January 1998

Canada

In early January 1998, a rare and devastating weather system exploded over central Canada. Freezing rain pelted the area for some eighty hours, toppling ice-laden trees and causing massive power outages. Southern Quebec and eastern Ontario suffered the full brunt of the storm. While the lights were out in Ottawa intermittently for days, outlying areas and much of the Quebec region were left in darkness for weeks, even months. Then the temperatures plummeted.

RCMP Inspector Liz Forsyth arrived back in Ottawa from London, England, in the late afternoon of Sunday, January 4.

She was looking forward to a week off following the intense and exhausting investigation into the murder of Natalie Guévin, Canada's chief trade commissioner in England.

Liz took a taxi to her home in Aylmer and watched, mesmerized, as the windshield wipers slapped at strange, heavy rain. It had grown dark. There was an oppressive silence as she tried to unlock her back door. The only sounds were rain falling on frozen snow and the odd creak of a heavy branch overhead. Liz's door lock was frozen shut. She was now very cold and more than a bit unnerved as she stood on the porch with her luggage at her feet. She felt about in her purse for her lighter and held it up to the lock. The flame looked pathetic in the darkness, but eventually the lock defrosted sufficiently to allow her into the house. She was wet through, and frozen. And the hydro was out.

She had planned to get something to eat and then go to bed to shake off her jet lag, but the food in her fridge was spoiling fast and the house seemed to be getting colder by the minute. The taxi driver had told her that this, apparently, was just the beginning. She blinked back unbidden tears, feeling suddenly very alone and frightened. Just as quickly, she told herself to "do something." Sometimes taking action, any action, was the way to start dealing with a situation. She remembered she had candles in the kitchen junk drawer. She managed to feel her way around and eventually got a fire going in the wood stove. Luckily she had bought some wood this year and it was neatly stacked in the garage. It had been meant for cozy winter evenings curled up on the couch, not as a means of survival. She piled as many logs as she could by the stove and made a sandwich of stale, semi-thawed bread and peanut butter. It was no use trying to call her landlord for assistance—he and his wife were on their annual Florida vacation. She piled blankets and her warmest coats onto the couch. Liz wasn't planning to trade the relative warmth of the living room for her freezing bedroom. Thanks to the jet lag, and despite the conditions, she quickly fell asleep.

England

Stephen Hay turned off his TV set but continued to stare at the blank screen. The detective chief inspector had been watching, with mounting concern, news reports of the severe ice storm affecting central Canada. He knew that his former colleague Liz Forsyth lived somewhere on the Quebec side of the Ottawa River, across from the Canadian capital, and that the area was being clobbered by a massive, unprecedented ice storm. He had been thinking rather a lot about Forsyth since her departure and was now becoming alarmed about her welfare. The BBC was reporting major power outages in Ontario and Quebec and running surreal footage of power transmission towers reduced to rubble by the weight of frozen rain.

He had grown what he would describe as "quite fond" of Liz Forsyth during her time in London. She was smart, funny, and a fine policeman. Woman. Whatever. Damned good at her job. They had become close during the Guévin investigation, and he had been sorry to see her go. They had both been a bit nervous and tentative at her leaving. He had driven her to Heathrow, given her a quick kiss on the cheek and a "bon voyage, Forsyth," before she headed through airport security. As he drove back to his home in Pimlico, the words "bon voyage, Forsyth" continued to mock him. *What a bloody stupid thing to say*, he thought. *But then*, he asked himself, *what* should *I have said? "Why don't you stay here, then?" That* would *have been bloody stupid. So what am I supposed to do now? Invite her to a vacation in the Bahamas or something?* Not exactly his style, and more than a bit presumptuous. Nothing had actually been said, let alone done. Although doubtless the Bahamas would look very appealing to her at the moment, if things were as bad as they seemed on television.

Hay wandered into the kitchen to refill his coffee, his thoughts on the ice storm. He finally decided to phone her and hoped that the phones would be working. He remembered that landlines usually remained in operation even when the electricity went out. It was just these nuisance mobiles that refused to function without electricity. Hay had obtained Liz's home phone number before she left—he wasn't completely daft. He lit a cigarette for courage and was reaching for the phone when unexpectedly it rang.

Superintendent Neilson's voice sounded strained, and he was speaking rapidly. "We have a body. A young woman on a pathway behind the Mallard Council Estate in Battersea."

Hay took down the particulars, called Detective Sergeant Wilkins, and crushed out his cigarette. As he slammed the front door shut he realized that it was the middle of the night in Canada anyway.

The coroner and her team, along with Dr. Shelly, the forensic pathologist, were on site when Hay and Wilkins met at the murder scene. In a doomed attempt to create a bit of green space behind the apartment towers, some bushes and a small plot of grass had been planted some time ago, obviously left untended ever since. The body had been discovered by a group of foreign students, who had seen a foot protruding from one of the bushes on the pathway. "I thought it was a mannequin," said a whey-faced Dutch youth when later interviewed. "We didn't believe it was real. We were, you know, sort of laughing. Then Adrien grabbed the foot and realized it was . . . flesh."

Already crime scene tape surrounded the site and unidentifiable people in white coveralls and masks were going about their gloomy business. The woman was lying on her side and, thought Wilkins, looked as if she had merely curled up and gone to sleep. She seemed quite peaceful. Long, dark hair draped her neck and shoulders. She was Caucasian, she was unclothed, and she was overweight. On her right hip was some sort of tattoo in dark blue ink. Wilkins squatted down for a closer look. No, not a tattoo. It appeared to be something like a signature—a word beginning with F, but the rest was illegible. A great many pictures of the mark were taken in case the ink, or whatever it was, rubbed off in transit. Or was rinsed away by the thin drizzle that had just begun.

DS Wilkins, regarding the peaceful features of the victim, murmured to himself that she didn't look dead.

"Oh, she's dead alright," said Dr. Shelly, with a small smile at Wilkins. "Look here." Hay and Wilkins drew closer as the doctor bent over and opened one of the girl's eyes. He held a magnifying glass to it, asking, "See those red dots?"

Wilkins nodded, and Hay said, "Asphyxial death, then?"

"Appears to be," agreed Shelly. "Petechiae," he said to Wilkins, referring to the red dots in the dead girl's eyes. "Clear sign of asphyxiation."

"So, strangulation?" asked Wilkins doubtfully. He had seen a couple of victims of strangulation already during his career, and they hadn't looked nearly so peaceful as this.

Shelly shook his head. "There are none of the grotesque facial distortions that occur with strangling," he said, shaking his head briefly in disgust. There were still sights that Shelly, despite his experience, found disturbing.

"Drowning's a possibility," he continued, "although we're some distance from any body of water and there's no indication the body has been moved. Of course that's your department. Could also be smoke inhalation, drug abuse . . ."

"Drug abuse?" asked Wilkins.

"Yes. Opioids can slow the system down so much that cause of death looks like asphyxiation. But there are no needle marks on her arms or legs, nor even in the places where users try to hide needle marks, like between the toes or fingers. But we'll need toxicology to definitively rule it out."

Shelly straightened up and arched his back, admitting to himself that his lower back pain was worsening.

"Smothering then?" pursued Hay.

"That's what I'm thinking at the moment," Shelly said, "although it's rare in adult victims. And pretty damned difficult if the person is conscious and struggling. We'll get more from the autopsy, of course."

"Anything under the fingernails?" Hay asked.

"Nothing visible. But we'll examine them under the microscope."

Hay nodded. "What's your best guess at time of death?"

"Probably sometime last night, but for now, at least, I can't be more precise," Shelly said. "It was a mild night, though." He glanced up at a sky that was now spitting out large drops of rain. "At least the weather shouldn't have influenced rigor."

With a nod from the coroner, several of the white-sheathed crew rolled the victim onto her back. The hair fell away from her face. She seemed very young to Hay, although he had realized that people in general seemed a lot younger to him these days. His own doctor seemed to be about twelve.

While the victim was completely naked, even devoid of jewellery, Hay noted that she must have usually worn a watch and had been left-handed—there was a strip of skin on her right wrist that was lighter than the rest. She wouldn't have gotten any type of tan in London in January. Had she been travelling?

Apart from the body, nothing appeared particularly striking about the crime scene. There were no nearby tire tracks; several sets of muddy footprints seemed to be smeared into one another; there was considerable disturbance of the mud around the body. *Perhaps*, wondered Hay, *when she was taking her clothes off? Or when they were being removed by someone else?* An intensive search of the vicinity was underway but nothing had yet been found to provide any idea of her identity. Eventually Hay and Wilkins left the experts to prepare the body for transport. There was little else they could do there.

Early the following morning, Paul Rochon scanned the headlines of the various British broadsheets and tabloids on his desk. Rochon, Acting High Commissioner of the Canadian High Commission in London, was usually the first in the office. Back when he was a very junior officer in the Canadian diplomatic corps, he'd hated walking into a full-blown crisis on arrival at the office and so chose to get in as early as possible. The habit hadn't left him throughout his decades of service.

This morning, the papers were full of the forthcoming council elections, the looming bus strike, and the British prime minister's visit to Southeast Asia. A couple of articles referred to the murder of an as-yet unidentified young woman behind a housing estate in South London. For some reason, that story stayed with him during the morning meeting of the programme heads and a mid-morning courtesy call from the newly arrived High Commissioner from Malaysia.

Rochon dialled the extension of the Head of Consular Affairs, Angela Mortenssen.

"Angela."

"Paul? Hi. What's up?"

"Just wondering about that woman you were telling us about in the morning meeting. The one who's been calling from, where, Montreal, yes? Trying to find her daughter?"

"Yes, well, there's not a lot we can do for her. The girl, Sophie Bouchard, hasn't registered with us and the mother doesn't even know if she's in England. She last heard from her when she was in Paris. Christmas Day."

"Did you see the item in the papers about a young

woman found murdered yesterday? Behind some council estate?"

"No," acknowledged Angela, "but we've been up to our eyeballs dealing with those Canadian kids involved in that car crash in Sheffield."

"Of course," said Paul.

Angela cocked her head. "What is it, Paul? Something about the missing girl?"

"I don't know," he replied slowly. "Do we have a physical description?"

"I think so. Let me check my notes." She pulled a sheet of paper from a desk covered in sheets of paper and sticky notes and continued. "Yes, about five foot two, long dark hair, brown eyes. Eighteen years old. A big girl, according to the mother."

"Okay, thanks," replied Rochon, and hung up the phone. He checked his phone list and placed a call to Scotland Yard.

Hay was poring over the crime scene reports from the homicide. Nothing seemed unusual in the surroundings except, of course, for the body of a naked young woman. An empty cigarette package, a used condom, a half-empty bottle of cola. Hay smiled wryly, wondering why the reporting officer chose to describe the bottle as half-empty. *Not half-full?* The shrill ringing of his desk-phone startled him from his philosophical ruminations.

"Chief Inspector, the Acting High Commissioner from the Canadian High Commission, a Paul Rochon, is on the line. Will you take it?"

Hay waited for the call to be transferred, and recognized Rochon's familiar, lightly accented voice.

"Detective Chief Inspector. Paul Rochon, from the Canadian High Commission."

"Of course," replied Hay, "and please, it's Stephen. How are you keeping?"

"Not bad, thanks. This 'acting' thing is keeping me busy since they sent High Commissioner Carruthers home last month."

"No doubt," said Hay. He'd heard that Carruthers had been unceremoniously recalled to Ottawa.

"What I'm wondering about," continued Rochon, "is this murder I've been reading about in the papers. Is it something that you're dealing with? It's just that, well, there's a woman in Canada who's been calling our Consular people and is urgently trying to track down her daughter. Apparently, the last she heard from the girl was at Christmas, and she was supposed to be heading to London. Have you identified the body yet?"

"No," replied Hay. "So far she's just a Jane Doe, as far as we know. You might be surprised how many of them there actually are. Do you have a description?"

Rochon passed on all the information that he had about the missing girl, which didn't amount to much.

"I realize there's nothing you can do," said Rochon. "We don't even know if she's in England."

"I'll keep my eyes open at any rate," said Hay.

"Okay," said Rochon. "Thank you, Stephen." Rochon hung up. He still felt uneasy. But what to do now? He sighed and went back to reviewing the draft political report on his desk.

Canada

A couple of days into the storm, Liz was still without power and loath to leave the house for fear of the fire going out. Driving was treacherous; she left her Honda in the garage, but she needed food and had to retrieve her mixed-breed dog, Rochester, from a nearby kennel. She managed these outings on foot, but walking seemed almost as dangerous as driving. Rochester was beside himself with joy when she claimed him, but she realized at once that he wasn't himself. He was anxious and needy, clinging to her, and by no means his usual bouncy, gregarious self. It took Liz a while to figure out what was wrong. Surely a dog would not be upset about a power failure or even by the lack of accustomed warmth in the kennel.

Liz realized what the problem was during one of their walks. It was eerily quiet as they slipped along the icy sidewalk. Then she recognized what was missing: the usual background hum of electricity running through the power lines. That was what was upsetting Rochester—the disappearance of something that, to his acute hearing, had been constant and familiar background noise.

She had checked several times on her closest neighbours, Marg and Bill Green. While Liz was at work, they often dogsat Rochester at their home, where he spent his time playing with their ageing poodle. The only reason Liz had resorted to placing Rochester in a kennel when she was unexpectedly dispatched to London in December was that the Greens had been visiting family in Nova Scotia.

An elderly couple, the Greens were resilient and self-reliant. They seemed to be faring better than many at present. They had two fireplaces and just under a cord of wood in their garage, so their house was kept quite warm. Being of an earlier and less privileged generation, they had taken to heart the caution that food and water should always be on hand in case of an emergency. They'd even had the foresight to purchase an emergency generator a few years back, so although Liz felt obliged to check on them from time to time, she realized they were probably doing better than she was. She invited them over one evening for a dinner of steaks cooked on the barbecue, trying to make a party of it, but she sensed they would probably be happier in their own home. It was, after all, warmer than hers. And so the evening had finished early.

"What a time to take a vacation," she muttered to herself. Rochester had followed her through the back door into the kitchen following their walk, and both of them were dripping onto the well-worn hardwood. She pulled off her boots and wiped the dog's paws on his towel. Rochester looked at her, faintly wagging his tail. He tipped his head, clearly asking, "Now what?" Liz patted him absently on the head and took off her ski jacket. She had several layers underneath, which were necessary even inside the house. She was being judicious with her store of firewood, having no idea how long the power would be off. The electricity came on occasionally, providing some relief for an hour or two, but would shut down again just as quickly.

At least the phones were still working. Headquarters had phoned to see if she was alright; they were phoning all the staff, which Liz appreciated. But no, she wasn't needed back in the office and could remain on "vacation." She was a bit disappointed by this but supposed it was prudent to stay home. Now that she had Rochester and some provisions, she wouldn't need to go out for some days. Emergency crews and the military were out trying to get trees off power lines and help people who were stranded; the emergency vehicles were the ones in need of the roads.

Liz had been able to reassure her mother in Calgary and her sister in Vancouver that she was safe and sound. She knew these things usually looked worse on television than they actually were, but even she had to admit that this was pretty bad. Normally healthy, upright bushes were bent at crazy angles, weighed down by layers of ice coating their branches. She had heard on her emergency radio that some enormous power-transmission towers around Montreal had collapsed from the weight of the ice and been rendered utterly useless. Tall trees in her own back yard had lost large limbs; she was grateful that her house was not directly underneath any of them. Nevertheless, the sound of branches cracking and crashing during the otherwise silent nights was frightening.

Not for the first time, she wished herself back in London. Granted, her work there had been exhausting, but more than rewarding. What had started as the murder of the Head Canadian Trade Commissioner at the High Commission in London had turned into a full-scale inquiry into international drug trafficking.

She wondered what Hay was doing at present. Certainly not freezing to death in the middle of an ice storm.

It had taken a couple of tries, but Hay finally got through to Liz on the phone.

"Forsyth," she answered, initially wondering if the office was calling to request her services after all.

"Liz, hello, it's Hay."

She had become quite accustomed to his accent during her time in London, and it was pleasant to hear again. Liz would have known him without the identification.

"Stephen," she replied, unaccountably relieved. "Great to hear from you."

"I've been watching the news and it looks like you're having some weather." Neither had she forgotten his predilection for understatement.

"Well, yes. I did tell you that you were better off in England, despite your continual griping about the rain."

He grinned. She sounded just the same. "How are you doing anyway? Do you have electricity?"

"Intermittently. I picked a hell of a time to take a vacation."

"You must be freezing."

"I have a wood stove, which is keeping me from totally seizing up. The roads are dreadful, so I'm mostly staying in or visiting the neighbours. How are you doing?"

"Fine, fine. Have a murder, which should keep me out of trouble. But seriously, you are okay, right?"

"Seriously, yes. But thanks so much for asking. Everything's fine, and Rocky—Rochester, that is—is with me. Still, this really is quite, well, scary. This climate is genuinely life-threatening. Don't know why people wanted to settle here in the first place."

Hay frowned. Forsyth was not easily frightened, but he noticed a slight tremor in her voice. "Well," he said, knowing he shouldn't but blundering on anyway, "perhaps when things settle down a bit we should meet up somewhere warm for a real vacation."

Liz inhaled quickly and was about to agree it would be a good idea when Hay rapidly interjected, "Maybe we could find an Interpol conference to attend or something."

The moment missed, Liz said that yes, that would be nice.

"So, you're alright," repeated Hay.

"Yes, yes, I'm alright."

"That's good. Well, just checking. Try to stay warm."

"I will, thanks, and, er, thanks for calling. Nice to hear your voice," she ventured.

"And yours," muttered Hay. He felt like an idiot.

"Talk soon, yes?" she said.

"Yes. Yes, absolutely. Goodbye."

"Goodbye."

Liz hung up and stared at the phone. Were all single people their age so socially inept? Was it just him? Was it her? Or were they each as bad as the other?

TWO
England

Acting Canadian High Commissioner Rochon was putting on his jacket, preparing to have lunch with his opposite number from the French Embassy. Unexpectedly, his Head of Consular Affairs, Angela Mortenssen, knocked on his door.

"Come in, Angela. What is it?"

"The woman who's been calling, Marie Bouchard, just phoned from Heathrow to tell us she's here. She's decided to try to find her daughter herself."

Paul stared at her in surprise, then said, "Offer her every assistance."

Angela nodded and turned towards the door. "Oh, and by the way," she said, turning back to Rochon. "Perry Henry is back and wants to see you."

"Oh no," groaned Rochon, sinking back into his chair. This was turning into a very bad day. Perry Henry was a good-natured schizophrenic from Oakville who enjoyed visiting England. Henry frequently came to the High Commission in order to complain that MI5 was after him. He had a particular liking for Paul Rochon, who always spoke kindly to him and gently escorted him off the premises. While the High Commission was often required to help Henry's parents with arrangements for his return to Oakville—at considerable expense to Mr. and Mrs. Henry—he would typically begin planning yet another trip to England as soon as he was back on Canadian soil.

"Please, Angela, can you deal with him?"

"Of course," she said. "Sorry, just kidding." Angela felt badly now, as she knew what a load Rochon was carrying. It had only been a joke.

"Very funny," he answered with a wry smile. "But thanks. He's the last thing I need right now."

It was, in fact, as Mme Marie Bouchard had feared. Her daughter, Sophie, lay dead and waxen in the morgue in London. While checking into her hotel, jet-lagged and fearful, she saw an item on the front page of a tabloid that had been left on the reception desk. Eyes blurring, she read of the unsolved murder of an unidentified young, large woman behind a housing estate.

Somehow Marie Bouchard finished checking in and

made it to her room. Sitting on the edge of the bed and feeling her heart pounding out of her mouth, she called Angela Mortenssen at the High Commission who told her that the High Commission would arrange with police for her to view the body, and send a vehicle to pick her up at her hotel.

Mme Bouchard took in none of the sights of London as the official vehicle transported her to the morgue, nor did she register anything of Angela Mortenssen's polite, discreet conversation as they sat in the back of the car. Marie Bouchard collapsed upon seeing her dead daughter and was escorted first to hospital, then back to her hotel.

Luciano Alfredo Carillo, Head Chef for the Canadian High Commission in London, was sharpening his knives in the quiet of the kitchen. Carillo took great pride in his knives, selected and collected during years of travelling and studying with his culinary gurus. It had been much quieter on the entertaining front since the erstwhile High Commissioner Carruthers and his harridan of a wife, Sharon, had been sent home under a very dark cloud.

The ends of Carillo's moustache tipped upward as he thought with satisfaction of their departure. It had been only last month, December, when all hell had broken loose in the normally decorous High Commission. The murder of poor Natalie Guévin, the revelation of the scandalous affair, the summoning of the Carruthers back to Ottawa— it seemed an age ago now.

Carillo inspected the edge of his filleting knife. Dissatisfied, he resumed sharpening it on his whetstone.

The Carruthers had done a great deal of entertaining—dinners, receptions, luncheons. Sharon Carruthers had clearly revelled in being the wife of the High Commissioner, rubbing elbows with British government ministers, visiting Canadian dignitaries, cultural icons, and exotic ambassadors. Carillo gave the whetstone a particularly savage swipe as he remembered the beautiful Sharon with her incessant complaints and demands. Of course, official entertaining was part of the job of a High Commissioner and his wife, but Sharon seemed interested only in showing herself and her latest outfit to advantage—and ordering him, Luciano Alfredo Carillo, around. He was still quite bitter about Mrs. Carruthers and reminded himself that, with any luck, he need never see her face again.

Paul Rochon, now Acting High Commissioner, wasn't doing much entertaining at all, reflected Carillo. The chef felt quite sorry for him, really; Rochon's normally heavy workload had doubled following the departure of Carruthers. While the odd rumour floated about concerning potential replacements for the former High Commissioner, Ottawa didn't seem in any particular hurry to name a successor. Not in Carillo's hearing at least. But his hearing was pretty good. As was that of the other domestic staff. Annie Mallett, for instance, the housemaid, seemed to pick up an extraordinary amount of information while dusting and polishing, although Luciano assumed that the quality of her information was probably about as reliable as her dusting.

Satisfied with the state of the filleting knife, Carillo turned his attention to his pride and joy, the chef's knife he had purchased for an exorbitant sum in Geneva. Carillo and his knife had enjoyed many culinary triumphs together and had suffered some mortifying failures. Luckily, the latter had been few, and his standing remained high with his professional colleagues. He held the perfectly weighted handle as though holding hands with a dearly beloved woman, and began working it on the stone.

What had he been thinking about? Oh yes, poor Paul Rochon. He was a nice man, with no wife to help out on the entertaining front. His hospitality allowance was mostly used for one-on-one lunches with his counterparts from other posts, government officials, journalists—the normal contacts that, as Carillo had learned, formed part of the network of diplomacy.

The engagements secretary, Mary Kellick, hadn't been replaced yet either. *Not that she'd been much use*, he thought, *poor cow*. Suicide, they said. Carillo's Catholic sensibilities were shocked, and he couldn't understand what could have driven a young woman over the edge like that. Probably Sharon Carruthers, he thought with a snarl.

Consequently, the work of the High Commission kitchen had all but ceased, but at least it meant that Carillo had time to experiment with some new recipes and do dull but important chores like, well, sharpening knives.

Absorbed in his work, Carillo almost dropped his precious knife when Annie Mallett, the housemaid, rushed in, her hard-soled shoes clattering on the tiles.

"They're back," she breathed.

"What?" said Carillo, irritated. Annie was alright but excitable. "Who's back?"

"Them coppers. The one with the lovely white hair and the other one, the young handsome one."

"What do they want here?" asked Carillo, mostly to himself.

"I don't know," replied Annie, her eyes wide with excitement. "Do you think someone else has been murdered?"

"Just like old times, eh, Sir?" asked Wilkins quietly.

Hay nodded. The surroundings of the Canadian High Commission felt familiar, which wasn't surprising. They had spent some time collaborating with the RCMP from what he had dubbed the "brandy-and-cigars" room while working on the Guévin murder. Since then, Hay had followed events in the diplomatic world with much greater interest than before. He knew that, as the investigation into Natalie Guévin's death was winding down, the Canadian High Commissioner, Wesley Carruthers, and his stunning bitch of a wife had been spirited back to Ottawa. Not surprising, mused Hay, since the High Commissioner had been having an affair with the victim. So now, while the Canadian government was casting about for a suitable replacement, Deputy High Commissioner Paul Rochon was filling in as Acting Head of Post. He had been looked at, briefly, regarding the Guévin murder, but over the course of the investigation Hay had developed considerable respect for the intelligent, forthright, and clearly overworked Rochon.

Hay was escorted to Rochon's office by one of the High Commission security staff. Despite the "Acting" designation, Rochon had decided to remain in his own office, deeming it unseemly to move his files into the High Commissioner's office.

Hay and Rochon greeted each other warmly as members of the grim fraternity sharing in the events of the previous month. Hay was also introduced to Angela Mortenssen, Head of Consular Affairs. He vaguely remembered meeting her during the Guévin investigation and also recalled that, at the time, she had been under some considerable pressure to repatriate Natalie's body back to Canada as quickly as possible. Guévin's father, Miroslav Lukjovic, was not a man to be easily ignored. Hay had learned at the time that consular officers were responsible for assisting Canadians in distress in foreign countries. Certainly Sophie Bouchard, who had been murdered, qualified.

"What do we know about her?" inquired Hay, after the usual pleasantries.

Rochon nodded to Mortenssen, who studied Hay through her bifocals. "As you already know, her name was Sophie Bouchard," she said. "She was from Montreal but apparently was travelling during her gap year. She was eighteen. She kept in regular touch with her mother, Marie, during her travels and had been on the road for about three months. Mother and daughter were very close."

Mortenssen, a veteran of consular affairs on her sixth foreign posting, frowned as she leafed through her notes. She was looking forward to retirement. Cases like this were becoming increasingly distressing.

"Sophie was planning to visit London next," she said. "Her mother had hoped she would call—collect, as per their arrangement—on New Year's Eve or Day. Sophie didn't call at that point, but Marie wasn't alarmed because Sophie said she would definitely call home on January 5, Mme Bouchard's birthday."

Consulting her notes again, she continued. "So since Christmas, Mme Bouchard—Marie—had heard nothing at all from Sophie. When her birthday came and went, she began to panic and called here a few times. I don't know what she thought she could achieve by coming here, nor what she thought she might find, but when a few more days passed without word from Sophie, she booked the earliest flight she could to Heathrow."

Mortenssen paused for breath and twirled a pen in her thick fingers. "Sophie hadn't registered with the High Commission, but then, very few people ever do—especially the young ones." She twitched her head at what she clearly considered a major lapse in judgment. "Of course we can't, and don't, and wouldn't even be legally allowed to keep track of the movements of Canadians abroad. And that's if we had anywhere near the resources. There was nothing we could do unless and until Sophie contacted the High Commission."

The High Commissioner's secretary knocked on the door, balancing a tray of coffee. Hay recognized the Canadian coat of arms on the cups. To Rochon's surprise, the tray also featured some buttery shortbread biscuits. Biscuits were not normally served to visitors. The High Commission chef, Luciano Alfredo Carillo, had sent them up when he learned the chief inspector was visiting again.

Carillo knew that the chief inspector recognized good food when he saw it. During the Guévin investigation,

Carillo had learned that the DCI had particularly appreciated the chef's lobster bisque and his watercress sandwiches. *Not*, thought Carillo, *like that High Commissioner and Mrs. Bloody High Commissioner, who didn't know a sauce béarnaise from a bottle of ketchup* . . . Carillo's thoughts continued indignantly down well-worn tracks littered with hot dogs and onion rings.

"So," said Rochon as Hay was leaving, "looks like you can't keep away from us Canucks."

Hay nodded grimly. He had been thinking the same thing.

The investigation into the murder of Sophie Bouchard was plagued with questions from the start. The police didn't know where she had been staying, how long she had been in London, if she knew her attacker, or what conceivable motive the murderer might have had. They didn't even know what had happened to her clothes. Some items of clothing had been found in the vicinity, all of it women's, but nothing large enough to fit the victim. It had been bagged for analysis anyway.

At least they had an identification. Sophie's mother was virtually speechless with grief and had provided the police very little apart from what they already knew. Sophie had been travelling on the continent and lost touch with her mother after her last contact from Paris, on Christmas Day.

Forensics had determined that the murder had taken place sometime during the night of January 4, prior to her discovery by the Dutch students the next morning. She had apparently been taken by surprise and then smothered.

There were no defensive wounds on the victim's hands, no microscopic scrapings under her nails, and no evident sexual interference. Toxicology results would take a while longer. The illegible mark on her hip had apparently been made by a blue, garden-variety permanent marker. Hay decided that the existence of the mark would be kept out of the press for the time being.

In the following days, Rochon and Hay remained in regular contact, despite, or perhaps due to, the lack of information in the case. During one of their conversations, Rochon invited Hay and DS Wilkins to the opening of an exhibit by a Canadian artist at a small gallery in Marylebone.

Rochon told Hay that Saskatchewan-based Louise Chapman was making a name for herself internationally, although she was little known in Canada. Wild, frightening landscapes. Oils. Edgy and uncomfortable to look at. Rochon admitted they would be the last thing he would have wanted in his living room. But Hay accepted the invitation on behalf of himself and Wilkins. If nothing else, he might have a better idea about Canada; perhaps it could be something intelligent—for a change—to discuss with Forsyth during a phone call.

Hay had just hung the phone up from his conversation with Rochon when it rang again. This time it was a young traveller; he provided the first solid information Hay had received on the Bouchard case. Bill White, a student from Kingston, Ontario, had bunked at a hostel in southwest London during the Christmas period—the same time that Sophie was staying there. The hostel was only about a half-mile from the murder scene.

White was now visiting Oxford and had only just heard about the murder. He had dialled the toll-free number immediately. No, he hadn't known Sophie well but she had seemed very nice, if a bit shy. Yes, he would come to the station and help in any way he could.

"She was already staying at the hostel when we arrived just after Christmas," said the lanky, ginger-haired young man after settling into a chair in the interview room. "I came in from Milan. I've been on the road for about six months. A few of us Canadians got to know one another a bit." He smiled, pointing to the frayed Canadian flag insignia on the shoulder of his black ski jacket. "Instant friendship" he added.

Sophie was, according to Bill, pleasant but quiet—very pleasant, in fact, and very heavy. There had been a party, perhaps on the night that Sophie disappeared, but Bill couldn't be sure. Some Australians (no, he only knew them as Bob and Bruce) had started playing guitar and harmonica one night, and before long a full-fledged party was underway. He didn't know how much Sophie had had to drink, much less how much he had consumed himself.

Bill thought she was drinking beer—at least that was what most people were drinking—and there seemed to be a lot of dope around. White was at pains to explain that he had not partaken of any drugs himself. He had gone to sleep very late and didn't know what time he would last have seen Sophie. And no, he had never seen her again. This was not unusual, he pointed out, as travellers came and went as they pleased.

White gave Hay a few more details, including the address

of the youth hostel where he and Sophie had both stayed. Hay requested a search warrant for the hostel as soon as White left, and went back to reviewing the latest reports on the case. One piece of information was new: according to British border control, Sophie Bouchard had travelled from Calais via the Chunnel to England on Sunday, December 28. *The festive season*, thought Hay irrelevantly, then resumed scrutinizing the file.

THREE
Canada

Laila Sergeyeva Daudova stood with a handful of others on Charlotte Street, as close to the gates of the Russian Embassy as allowed. She scrunched her coat and woollen scarf tightly under her chin, holding the picture in her other hand. It was freezing cold. She had thought that Grozny was cold, but there was something in this Ottawa dampness that cut straight through her. The freezing rain had stopped, but much of the city was at a standstill. Nevertheless, she believed deeply in what she was doing, and so did her few compatriots from the tiny Chechen community in Ottawa. A few representatives from.Independence United rounded out their number.

The eight-by-ten-inch picture that Laila was holding up to the impassive face of the Russian Embassy was that of her brother, Bula Sergeyevich Gavrikov. He should have been with her and Rasul, safely in Canada, but Bula had disappeared only days before the couple fled Chechnya two years earlier. She hadn't heard a word from him since.

The others here were in similar circumstances: the tiny old woman, dressed in black, holding a picture of her granddaughter; the angry-looking, bullet-headed young man holding a picture of another angry-looking, bullet-headed young man; the beautiful young woman with the startling blue eyes, holding a picture of her missing husband. The people from Independence didn't have pictures, but they carried large placards reading, "Shame for the Disappearances in Chechnya" and "Freedom for all Chechens." The Independence United representatives rounded out the small group of protesters that had been rallying here for months, whenever they could manage. Today was the first day they had been able to make it out since the ice storm.

Laila was glad that her husband, Rasul, had managed to get to his job at the parking lot today—not that she expected there would be much business in these conditions. Traffic was quiet and the driving dangerous. Since her arrival in front of the Russian Embassy, Laila had already seen two cars skid, quite out of control, along Charlotte Street. She was glad that her husband would be otherwise occupied and not so concerned about her attending the demonstration.

Suddenly she heard a loud pop and her body was on fire. Seconds later, she lay dying on the pavement, her blood pooling on the icy Ottawa sidewalk.

Liz had a couple of days of "vacation" left when it was cut short by a phone call from her superintendent.

"There's been a shooting, a demonstrator outside the Russian Embassy. Shot dead. Just under an hour ago. Can you get there now? You know all about embassies, right?"

"Of course I can come in. But I hardly know 'all about embassies.'"

"Close enough," replied the Super. "Embassy Protection is all over it, of course, but I want you there."

Liz agreed—this was exactly the sort of case in which her department, Federal Investigations, would take the lead. Embassy Protection was not accustomed to homicide and was, at the best of times, chronically under-resourced. Liz jotted down the particulars and presently was guiding her Honda over the Champlain Bridge towards Ottawa.

The crime scene was humming when Liz parked on Charlotte Street outside the stark exterior of the Russian Embassy. The coroner and forensics team were already there, along with numerous uniformed police officers. The members of the press seemed to have sprouted as quickly as the demonstrators had melted into the background. Officers were manning the perimeter of the scene.

Liz inspected the young woman's body. She was wearing a down-filled jacket, a long, black skirt, low-heeled, rubber-soled boots, and a heavy scarf wrapped around her head and neck. She had been a very pretty woman, probably in her mid-twenties and, despite her bulky clothing, appeared slight and short in stature. From the pattern of the blood, it appeared that the shot had hit her square in the back. Nearby lay a sort of picket sign, with the image of a young, dark-haired man on it. Something was written underneath but it was in an unintelligible script, at least to Liz.

A great deal of measuring was going on as the experts tried to gauge the trajectory of the bullet. Two police constables were struggling to interview a Russian Embassy security guard, evidently with little success as the man simply alternated between shrugging his shoulders and shaking his head. Several police officers were attempting to keep the press away from the scene and behind the tape. Suddenly three embassy officials, all men, materialized; the one in the middle, clearly the superior, was flanked by his staffers. A police officer pointed them towards Liz, who was still scrutinizing the body and its immediate vicinity.

The Russian officials introduced themselves. "I am Vladimir Kraznikov, ambassador of the Russian Federation. This is my personal assistant, Piotr Leskov, and the embassy's cultural attaché, Stanislav Ivanov."

Liz thought it would be prudent to get the spellings later.

"Ivanov saw the shooting from his window," said the ambassador in heavily accented English. "He was obviously not working," he said without a hint of a smile, "and saw the woman fall."

Ivanov took up the story. "It is true—I was watching the demonstration. This morning the group was particularly small but comprised the usual people who come. This was the first demonstration since the storm."

Liz was surprised to hear a trace of a British accent. *Perhaps he had learned his English from a Brit?*

"Where is your office?" asked Liz, with a glance towards

the front of the building. Ivanov pointed to a small window facing Charlotte Street.

"They were very quiet," continued Ivanov. "They all looked cold. But they feel they must come because they think the Russian government has kidnapped their loved ones. If only they understood that the disappearances are due to the Chechen authorities themselves—"

"Thank you, Stanislav," interrupted the ambassador, who clearly thought his cultural attaché had gone far enough.

"So you recognized the demonstrators?" pursued Liz.

"Oh yes," answered Ivanov. "This woman," he nodded towards the body, "is always here. She complains that her brother disappeared in Chechnya. He was meant to be coming with her to Canada."

"Do you have the names of these people?" asked Liz.

With a quick look at the ambassador, Ivanov nodded.

"Come in and we will tell you what we know," said Kraznikov. There was little else she could do here, and the body would be readied for transport soon.

"Thank you," she said, walking into the building with the ambassador, his cultural attaché, and his broad-shouldered, unsmiling "personal assistant."

By the time Liz left the embassy, she had a short list of the demonstrators' names, the correct spelling of those of her interlocutors, and a mild headache from the powerful Russian cigarette she had been offered. At least they still allowed smoking inside their building. The Russians were definitely going up in Liz's estimation.

The body had disappeared by the time Liz started

her car and began steering towards the RCMP office on Cooper Street, which housed the Federal Investigations Department. Apart from the glistening remnants of the ice storm, it was a typically gloomy, mid-winter Ottawa afternoon. Dirty, glittering snowbanks lined the sidewalks. The cars that braved the streets already had their lights on, and it wasn't yet four o'clock.

She went directly to her superintendent's office. He looked even more rotund than usual, and his face was ruddier. The Super always gave Liz the impression that he was about to explode—not in anger, as he was a very even-tempered man—but something like a birthday balloon that had been filled rather too enthusiastically. Liz occasionally wondered how the good man passed his annual physical. She didn't recognize the other man in the room, a thin, balding, bespectacled person whom the Super identified as Lawrence Fletcher from the Canadian Security Intelligence Service. Liz noticed that Fletcher's prominent nose seemed to be itchy, as he scratched it vigorously from time to time during the interview.

Of course, thought Liz, CSIS *would be involved in this.*

Fletcher took no part in the ensuing discussion of events. Occasionally he took a note and spent much of his time regarding Liz and the superintendent as though they were, in fact, suspects in the case.

"I'd like to request Ouellette," she said as the discussion drew to a close. "He knows 'all about embassies,' just like me." Sergeant Gilles Ouellette had been her invaluable side-kick during the Guévin investigation in London.

The Super nodded and picked up the phone.

The following day, which had largely been spent running down leads and sifting through evidence, Liz stopped for a late dinner at a small Italian restaurant in Ottawa's Byward Market. She was delaying her return home; the power was still unpredictable there, and she wasn't looking forward to returning to the uncertain climate of her living room. The restaurant, A Tavola, was clearly upscale and updated, not like those she had known in her youth, with their red-and-white checked tablecloths, candles housed in Chianti bottles, and "Santa Lucia" belting out from the sound system. This one sported a good deal of black and chrome, the candles were short and fat, and the menu included several items few Italians would recognize.

She had been there once or twice before, and the chicken Parmigiana was to her liking. Liz was one of those people who, once finding a dish they like, continue to order the same thing until the restaurant goes out of business. She understood that there were people who ordered something different every time they visited a restaurant, but could only conclude they were of a different species.

Not that her mind was on chicken Parmigiana anyway. She was thinking about Laila Daudova, the Chechen woman shot dead outside the Russian Embassy. The Russians had been helpful in handing over the names of the "regulars," as they called them—those who routinely turned up to protest the disappearance of loved ones in Chechnya. She had asked at the time if it was a coincidence that the names of the women ended with an "a" while the men's seemed to end with "ev" or "ov," and learned that this was, in fact, the way that masculine and feminine Russian surnames were constructed. The cultural attaché had launched into a detailed explanation of how Russian middle names actually meant "son of" or "daughter of," but the ambassador had impatiently cut him short.

RCMP officers were tracking down the "regulars" and conducting preliminary interviews, and Liz was forming the impression that they were a truculent and uncooperative lot. The protesters from Independence United hadn't provided much information either, and Sergeant Gilles Ouellette, who in typical fashion had swotted up on the situation in Chechnya as soon as he was assigned to the case, had expressed disdain at how little the professional protestors apparently knew about the Chechen wars.

Liz smiled to herself, sipping her Cabernet. There was a reason she had requested Ouellette for this case. He was an officer who gave one hundred percent every time and was extremely bright, professional, and thorough. She would have to be careful with him, though. She had learned during her years with the police that the more diligent and conscientious the officer, the greater the risk that he or she could be taken advantage of.

Some superiors routinely abused their best officers, overloading them to the breaking point, because they knew that the loyal officer would make sure the work was done, no matter what the personal cost. And that made the boss look good. It was the enthusiastic, dedicated young officers who ran the greatest risk of burnout, or worse.

Liz had known a young woman who fit into that category—highly intelligent and sensitive. That woman had unwittingly found herself working for a succession of brutal superiors. She had lasted about ten years; then she gave up her career before she lost the remainder of her self-respect. Now the woman owned a popular restaurant in Kingston.

Liz knew that she had been very lucky with her own bosses. Some, of course, had been better than others, but she hadn't personally run into any that were particularly callous. Liz had been fortunate, and she knew it. As a woman, she knew that some of her generation and gender were suffering insidious forms of harassment and bullying.

Her current Super, however, was delightful to work with, an absolute pro who was both incisive and thoughtful. He could always be trusted to offer well-considered advice; at the same time, he trusted Liz's instincts and investigative methods. She took another swallow of wine and returned her thoughts to the case at hand. She and Ouellette would interview Laila's husband, Rasul, the next morning. Rasul Daudov had been uncommunicative with the uniformed officers conducting the first interview but reportedly had seemed genuinely distraught and grief-stricken by his wife's death.

Other than these people—the husband, the demonstrators, and perhaps the Russians—who could have wanted to kill Laila Sergeyeva Daudova? Of course, the entire Chechen community (which numbered about twenty as far as Liz could tell) would be spoken with. Might it have been mistaken identity? Was someone else the target? Or—she was really stretching here—was this an attempt to embarrass Canadian security for some reason? Her chicken arrived, on a bed of al dente pasta tossed with marinara sauce and Parmesan, and surrounded by steamed root vegetables. She thanked the waiter and cut into the tender chicken. Of course the shot seemed to have been a good one. Square in the back, right through the heart, according to forensics. It was either a brilliant shot or a very bad mistake.

Liz realized that she was very happy to be back at work. And the pasta was good.

What about the Russians, though? These protestors must have been a major thorn in their sides for years. Was there something particular about Laila that might have inspired the Russians to risk provoking a major international incident? If that were the case, this was way out of her league. A homicide, fine, but some intelligence and security matter? She was losing her appetite quickly, although the Parmigiana was certainly up to standard. Anyway, that was not her business, she decided. She would continue to do the police work to the best of her ability; there were others who could deal with the spooky stuff. Like that Lawrence character from CSIS—Lawrence, of course, not Larry. He had looked pretty spooky himself, apparently thinking it would be unprofessional to crack a smile throughout their entire meeting.

Liz found herself wondering how Hay would approach this case. He had been in pretty much the same situation during the Guévin murder at the Canadian High Commission in London, hoping that the murder was an isolated matter that could be solved by solid police work, rather than some ethereal intelligence matter that would never be explained satisfactorily. He had told her of those feelings during the evening they went to the Bull's Head pub in London, the day after they had solved the High Commission murder. It had been a wonderful evening, she remembered, full of laughter and exhaustion and the sort of inside jokes one only shares after years of friendship. But their friendship had been only a couple of weeks. She had been sorry to leave.

She was also sorry to get back home to Aylmer. As she had suspected, the power was off again. She collected Rochester from the Greens and he, too, was a bit subdued as they entered the dark house.

FOUR

Canada

Rasul Daudov opened the door to his visitors. The tiny, sparsely furnished apartment in a three-storey walk-up in the east end of Ottawa at least had heat and electricity. Daudov was short and thick-set, with dark, almost-black eyes and a complexion that, in earlier times, would have been described as "swarthy." He was visibly upset, his eyes red-rimmed and swollen. He regarded Liz and Ouellette with thinly veiled suspicion.

Following introductions, Liz asked Daudov about Laila.

After complaining that he had already spoken with the police, he said haltingly, "She was very beautiful. Kind.

Generous. Look. Here is picture." He took a small photo in a plain five-by-seven frame from the table and handed it to Liz. A lovely woman with eager, bright eyes stared back at her. "I take that just before we leave Chechnya," said Daudov sadly. Abruptly he added, "Russians did this, sure." He nodded to himself as he spoke.

"We don't yet know who did this, Mr. Daudov. That's why we're here. Why do you suspect the Russians?"

Daudov snorted. "They hate us, generally. They kill our countrymen in Chechnya. And Laila—she would not stop trying to find brother." Daudov was becoming agitated; Liz noticed his accent grew heavier and his English more laboured.

"When did you and Laila come to Canada, Mr. Daudov?"

"Two years," he said slowly, gazing steadily at Liz. She realized that the question had made him extremely nervous and that he was clenching and unclenching his fists rapidly.

"We are not from the Immigration Department, Mr. Daudov. We just want to find out what happened to your wife."

Daudov looked at her steadily, then seemed to relax as he took a short breath.

"So you left Chechnya with your wife two years ago . . ."

Daudov shook his head. "No. Almost three years ago. Took long time to get here. Many countries. We marry here in Canada," he said—somewhat proudly, thought Liz. "Bula should come with us but disappeared few days before we left."

"Bula was her younger brother?" asked Ouellette.

"Yes. Younger brother." Daudov swung his gaze towards

the young sergeant. "Bula always want to come to West. He liked travel. Went to neighbour countries. Sometimes even South Asia, I think. He wanted to come to West and then he was gone. We waited. Finally we could wait no more. We had to leave or chance would be lost."

Ouellette figured there must have been one very interesting story behind the Daudovs' move to Canada, but, as Forsyth had pointed out, she and Ouellette didn't work for Immigration. He noticed that a few books on speaking English and a picture book on Canadian history lay on the floor. It appeared to Ouellette that the Daudovs intended to become good Canadians, no matter how they had gained entry. He went back to his note-taking.

"Can you think of anyone who would have wanted to hurt your wife, Mr. Daudov?"

"Russians."

"How about apart from the Russians? Did she know many people here?"

"No, not really. We know some Chechens. She know other demonstrators a bit."

Liz went over the list of regulars she had been provided by the Russian Embassy, and Daudov told them what little additional information he had. He mentioned that Laila had been particularly fond of a Mrs. Umarova, an elderly woman and fellow demonstrator.

Ouellette asked what Daudov's movements had been on the day of the killing. As Ouellette had anticipated, the other man quickly became angry. "Why you want to know about me? I say all this to police yesterday already. Why you not talk to Russians?" demanded Daudov.

"Please, Mr. Daudov," interjected Liz, "we need to know."

Daudov stared at her for a moment, then sighed heavily. "I was working my job at parking lot. Montreal Road. All day."

"Did anyone see you there?"

"Very quiet day. Not many cars because of storm. But I tell you one thing: If I had not been there, I would be fired. Easy to find parking lot attendants. I need to keep job."

Liz and Ouellette learned from ballistics that the bullet that killed Laila Daudova had been fired from some type of assault rifle. The lethal bullet, measuring 7.62 by 39 millimetres, was used primarily in weapons from Eastern Europe and Russia.

"Including," asked Ouellette, "the AK-47?"

"Yes," replied the bespectacled ballistics expert, shifting his gaze from Liz to the sergeant. "The Avtomat Kalashnikova fires this type of bullet. The AK-47 is widely used and very reliable—but not very accurate. The shooter must have been highly skilled to shoot from across the street and hit the woman full in the back."

"It's a semi-automatic, yes?" asked Liz.

The spectacles nodded. "But also capable of firing a single shot."

"And no shell casing was found," Liz said.

"No. The shooter must have picked it up before he fled. He knew what he was doing. In fact," he continued, "I'm going out on a bit of a limb here, but I would guess the shooter knew this gun quite well. They're not the easiest things for targeting and he was very accurate." He gave a short nod towards the corpse. "It would be a lot easier to pull this off with a weapon that you knew."

Liz and her sergeant were silent, deep in thought, as they took a taxi to their appointment at Foreign Affairs on Sussex Drive. They had abandoned the idea of taking the squad car due to the virtual impossibility of parking anywhere near the Pearson Building. They entered the building's spacious lobby and were greeted by an officious but nervous young woman who escorted them to the office of an assistant deputy minister.

The ADM was a short man with a puffy face, haggard expression, and ghastly tie. There they were joined by the director general of the Eastern European Bureau. She was a stocky woman dressed all in navy blue: an ill-fitting jacket and skirt, navy hose, and flat shoes. Two younger officers were also in attendance, both wearing colourful bow ties.

During the meeting, Liz and Ouellette learned more about the small Chechen community in Canada and confirmed some historical details about that troubled region. There was no firm information about the size of the Chechen community in Ottawa and area, and the Chechens generally kept a low profile. This was probably because many had entered the country illegally.

Ouellette noted that the Chechens did not even appear to interact much among themselves. Those who regularly demonstrated outside the Russian Embassy on Charlotte Street didn't seem to spend much time together apart from the demonstrations. At least that was what the preliminary interviews had suggested. Of course, none of these people were suspects anyway, having been with Laila at the time of the shooting. At the same time, they seemed unable or unwilling to help the police determine who might have wanted her dead.

Liz and Ouellette also learned more about Independence United, an organization for which the departmental officials expressed some disdain. "A rent-a-crowd," said the director general. Ouellette nodded at this, as the description coincided with his own assessment of the organization. The Canadian chapter was headquartered in Ottawa and was affiliated with a number of like-minded organizations. Independence United routinely allied itself with any group seeking self-determination, however worthy, or flimsy, the cause. *At least*, thought Ouellette, *that group might be amusing to talk to*. Ouellette had never been one to sign up for causes, no matter how worthy they might be; he was not a joiner. His only "cause," although he would never have thought of it that way, was to make sure the bad guys were put behind bars.

FIVE
England

Once a fortnight, DCI Stephen Hay joined his brother Keith and his domestic goddess of a wife, Helena, for dinner. Helena adored both the Hay brothers and had been trying for years to set up her brother-in-law Stephen with any number of her single, widowed, or divorced girlfriends. In one particularly desperate attempt, she had tried to introduce him to one who was merely unhappily married. None of these efforts had paid off, however, and, in recent years Helena had resigned herself to cooking for just the brothers every couple of weeks.

Helena was an excellent cook and, in her more honest

moments, recognized that her love of entertaining was mostly as an excuse to show off. She was privately irked by the bad reputation English cuisine had elsewhere—especially in Europe—and was doing her bit to prove the continentals wrong. Whatever the motivation, Helena was a gracious hostess, and tonight the three of them were sitting down to a starter of puff pastry with warm brie and raspberries.

"Delicious, Helena, as always," said Stephen. While he often dreaded these fortnightly visits, he invariably enjoyed them once he was there. Keith nodded and gave an "mmmph" of assent as he demolished buttery layers of pastry.

Their conversation began as it usually did, with polite inquiries regarding Helena's bad hip (which was "much the same"), Keith's gout (which seemed to be getting worse), and Stephen's arthritic knee. This evening, as on every previous such evening, Keith opined that this had doubtless been brought on by his brother's misspent youth playing football.

When they were seated in the dining room and presented an enormous casserole of boeuf à la bourguignonne, fresh baguette, and roasted vegetables, Helena could contain herself no longer.

"So Stephen, that body I've been reading about behind the council estate—that's on your patch, isn't it?" Helena had a curious, hurried manner of speaking and rarely stopped to take a breath, but she was, in fact, correct about this. Battersea was normally his "patch." He had been assigned to the investigation at the High Commission only because the Yard had thought him the right man for the job.

"Yes," answered Hay simply.

"But they're saying in the papers that it was a young woman who was very large and foreign, wasn't she," said Helena, more as a statement than a question.

"Yes," Hay repeated. "But you know, Helena, that I can't give you any details of the investigation."

Indeed she did know, as she had been told this many, many times.

Keith Hay, a chemical engineer, believed himself to be the only one in his family not fascinated by violent crime. Their father had been a uniformed officer until retirement, his brother Stephen was a DCI, and his own lovely wife seemed to think she was Miss Marple. Why her well-paid job as a pharmacist wasn't enough for her, Keith didn't know. He took a sip of wine and focused on the beef and pearl onions.

"Yes of course I know that Stephen but it's been in all the papers and on the news. Will she be doing a televised appeal? I always think that must be so hard to sit up there in front of all those cameras and beg for information about what happened to a loved one. I saw one a couple of weeks ago by the parents of the baby son who went missing somewhere it was very sad I hope they catch that one." Helena paused for breath, inhaled, then continued. "*Have* you had many tips?"

Detective Chief Inspector Hay sighed, mutely appealing for help from his brother, but Keith appeared fascinated by the plate in front of him.

"I really can't tell you that, Helena. Yes, there have been tips. No, we still don't know who did it."

Oh, there have been tips alright, he thought. So far, many were from the same people who *always* phoned in tips, about any murder, any robbery, any crime. People who apparently had a great deal of time on their hands and very little to do but try to involve themselves in police investigations. Many had theories they would be happy to share with the police. None had actual information. These people were, of course, wasting police time, but they were rarely charged because, well, that really would be a waste of police time.

"She was Canadian, they say," continued Helena. "You worked with the Canadians on that last case; they seem to get into an awful lot of trouble over here, don't they? A Liz something, wasn't it?" She threw a quick look at Hay. *He had,* thought Helena, *mentioned this Liz person's name frequently during their last dinner—well, frequently for Stephen. Twice, anyway.*

"That's right," said Stephen. "This is lovely, Helena. What herb is it that I'm tasting in the sauce?" Having engaged the charming Helena on one of her favourite subjects, he managed to dodge other police-related matters for the rest of the evening, and even Keith managed to rejoin the conversation before dessert (cherries jubilee) was served.

Having reluctantly turned down the offer of more excellent burgundy, Hay drove back to his home. His father's will had given Keith the money, Stephen the property. Both of them had found this a good arrangement. Hay parked in his small garage, then let himself into his empty house.

It was a small gallery, in the heart of Marylebone. Hay and Wilkins arrived shortly after six and were greeted warmly by Acting High Commissioner Paul Rochon. In attendance was the young Canadian artist whose work was being celebrated, and a waiter offering sparkling wine. Several dozen guests had already arrived at the opening reception and were chatting in groups or intently studying the paintings. The artist, Louise Chapman, didn't remotely resemble what Hay expected of an internationally renowned artist. There was nothing at all flamboyant about her: she wasn't swathed in shawls, nor was she sporting a mass of unkempt hair and enormous earrings. Hay wondered briefly how and why he had come up with such a stereotype in the first place. Louise Chapman was, in fact, a small and plain-looking young woman who appeared somewhat alarmed by her own success.

Wilkins engaged her in conversation while Hay wandered off to examine the paintings. They were, as Rochon had commented, very jarring and brutal winter landscapes. *Not Constables, at any rate*, thought Hay, referencing the romantic painter of a bucolic, historic England. He wondered if this was how many Canadians saw their land: unforgiving, frozen, life-threatening. The paintings were somehow full of hatred. Occasional tiny figures appeared in the paintings; small and virtually insignificant, the figures somehow reminded Hay of the one in Munch's famous "Scream." The paintings were definitely of good quality—the brushstrokes were fine and nuanced and the use of colour superb—but after studying the collection he found himself a bit depressed. He understood why Rochon didn't want one in his living room. He wondered if these paintings were how Forsyth might be feeling in her unheated home in Quebec at that moment, and he felt a tightening in his gut.

Wilkins had moved on to chat to a clutch of attractive women in the room. *Has he even looked at the paintings?*

wondered Hay. He noticed that Rochon was speaking to three young men on their way out of the gallery. They were rather loud and smiling: one, noticed Hay, was somewhat pear-shaped while another had a pockmarked face. The third was dressed completely in black, including what looked like a modified fedora, and had affected an artistic pose. Having said their farewells, Rochon and Hay caught up with each other again.

"Good turnout, I think," said Hay.

"Not bad," agreed Rochon.

"I didn't realize that Embassies, er, sorry, High Commissions did this sort of thing as well."

"Oh yes," said Rochon. "We have quite an active cultural programme at the High Commission—well, all our posts abroad do. We try to assist Canadian artists in their overseas ventures, and it's a good way to raise Canada's profile. In fact, one of those guys," he indicated the young men just leaving, "is hoping to inveigle us into supporting his work at some point. They're all art students at some college in southern Ontario. But he won't have much of a chance—he doesn't have an impresario or anyone who's willing to represent him or finance his stuff. We don't go that far to show the flag," he added with a grin.

Hay smiled back. He always found it interesting to learn the range of things with which embassies occupied themselves.

Rochon continued. "Ah, there's our Programme Head for Cultural Affairs, Sarah Farell." Paul raised his eyebrows in that subtle manner that conveys not only acknowledgement, but a request from across a room, without the involvement of any spoken language. The woman, understanding Rochon's meaning perfectly, quickly joined them.

"Sarah, this is Detective Chief Inspector Hay of the Yard," said Rochon. "I was just explaining our cultural programme to him."

"Yes," said Hay, lowering his voice a little. "I'm not sure that I like these paintings much, but I recognize that they are very good."

Sarah laughed. "That's not the first time I've heard that this evening. But serious collectors seem to like them very much—and Louise is such a sweetheart, so it's nice to give her a bit of a boost."

Presently, Wilkins joined Hay and they made their way to Wilkins's Escort. "What did you think of the paintings?" inquired Hay a bit sarcastically, and to his surprise learned that Wilkins had inspected them in some detail. He actually liked them quite a bit, or so he said, and was thinking of buying one for his girlfriend, Gemma, for her forthcoming birthday. Whether this spoke to Wilkins's sophisticated taste in art or to the state of his relationship with Gemma was unclear.

During the review next morning, DCI Hay and his team attempted to posit scenarios about the homicide. The problem was that in order to create a decent hypothesis, they needed some decent information. There was very little so far. It seemed that the victim, Sophie Bouchard, had been killed at the scene, not dumped there after her murder. One young constable helpfully pointed out that had she been dumped there after death, the offender must have been a very large person indeed.

No one from the Mallard Council Estate could confirm that they had seen or heard anything unusual on the night of the murder. Sophie had been found about a half-mile from her hostel. The Council Estate was on a regular bus line and, while one of the drivers normally on the afternoon shift remembered seeing Sophie, he could not remember exactly when, or if anyone had been with her. It was, it seemed, her size that made her stand out.

Some of the young people were still staying at the hostel, but some, including Bill White, had moved on, having left their contact information with the police. Others had neglected to do so.

Mme Bouchard had agreed readily to a televised appeal. Her daughter, Sophie, had been dead for some days and it seemed that little, if any, progress had been made. The mother appeared in front of the cameras, tearful but determined, pleading with viewers in her French Canadian accent to help find the man—she said "man," convinced it could not be a woman—who had killed her only daughter. A tips line had been set up, and several hundred calls were made to police within the first couple of hours, keeping many officers employed but yielding little useful information.

At least that was Hay's opinion, as he sifted through the reports sent to him for review. The evident pranksters and publicity seekers had been weeded out, but what remained wasn't enough to solve a murder. Someone had seen a very large girl with long, dark hair early on the afternoon of January 4 at a café not far from the Mallard Council Estate. The tipster said it was the girl's size that had struck her, as she'd earlier been reading a newspaper account about the problem of obesity in the United States. At the time, she'd wondered if the girl was American. A young woman who'd been staying at Sophie's hostel at about the time of the murder called from Edinburgh, confirming that Sophie had been very pleasant but kept to herself. There were a few other reports of sightings; all would be followed up, but no solid leads had surfaced.

The one thing that particularly stood out was the preliminary toxicology report, which stated that Sophie had ingested Rohypnol, a substance known as a "date-rape" drug. Ironically, no rape or any other type of sexual assault had taken place. No evidence of sexual activity at all had turned up. *So*, wondered Hay, *she was drugged and murdered . . . but why?* Clearly it was not a sex crime—at least not like anything he had seen before. Forensics also found two fine grey fibres under the girl's jaw. Was it from whatever had been used to smother her?

As a young woman bunking in hostels, she was an unlikely robbery victim, although her watch was missing, along with the clothes she'd been wearing and a green purse, which her mother had described to police. Her large grey knapsack had been locked up at the hostel, but it contained only items of clothing and toiletries. Drugs? *Maybe*, he thought, although nothing but the Rohypnol, and alcohol, had turned up in her system. She had no criminal record back in Canada and, as far as Hay knew, hadn't attracted the attention of police during her European travels.

A personal motive, then, was possible, and police were continuing to interview anyone they could find who had come into contact with her. The Royal Canadian Mounted

Police were interviewing her acquaintances back in Montreal. Hay had been a bit disappointed to learn that Forsyth had not been assigned to his case, but he knew she was too senior to be doing such routine work. Anyway, she was stationed in Ottawa, not Montreal. Although he had to admit to himself that he wasn't really sure how far apart the two cities were.

All of which left him with, essentially, nothing. There was always the chance that this was a random killing—someone going off the rails and lashing out—but this murder seemed far too methodical for that. There was the Rohypnol, the lack of evidence, and that strange mark on her hip.

Hay swirled some cold coffee around in his mug, his eyes unfocused. He turned his attention to the file containing photographs of the mark. It appeared to be a short word beginning with *F*. But it didn't appear to be the word that immediately sprang to his mind. He looked at the photos from several angles, as he had already done numerous times, and put them back in the folder.

He had to leave soon anyway. Mme Marie Bouchard was accompanying her daughter's body back to Canada that evening. He felt he should be there to say goodbye.

When he returned to his house in Pimlico that evening, he saw the answering machine light was flashing, indicating one new message. He threw off his coat, kicked off his shoes, and lit a cigarette. He switched on the machine and leaned against his kitchen counter. *Damn*, he said to himself, recognizing the accent.

"Hi Stephen. Er, Liz here. Guess you're working, eh? It's pretty busy here—we've got a case of a killing outside the

Russian Embassy in Ottawa. You might have read about it. Anyway, hope you're well. Take care. Bye. Er, yeah. Bye."

Hay checked the time of the message and looked at his kitchen clock. Early afternoon in Ottawa. She would doubtless be working. Damn, but this time difference was annoying.

SIX
Canada

In accordance with procedure, an integrated task force had been set up at RCMP headquarters to investigate the murder of the young Chechen demonstrator Laila Daudova. In addition to Liz and Ouellette, there was an assortment of uniformed RCMP officers and plainclothes detectives, plus two members of the Ontario Provincial Police and a representative of the Ottawa-Carleton Police Department. Liz knew a few of the RCMP officers but hadn't met the others before. One man she recognized—a square-shaped, powerfully built man called Greg Gibson—worked for the Embassy Protection Branch. The task force squashed into a small room on the second floor and reviewed the case to date.

Laila Daudova had been shot in the back from across the street, and her assailant had melted away immediately after firing the fatal shot. An expert marksman. Who took the shell casing with him. A trained killer, perhaps? With some sort of assault rifle, probably from the former Soviet bloc, possibly an AK-47. No footprints had been found in the area—the crusty, slippery snow had seen to that. Apart from a few broken branches—which might well have been snapped due to the ice storm—nothing indicated that anyone had been lurking there. Nothing but the trajectory of the bullet. Police had combed the area but came up empty-handed.

Liz learned that there were government cameras in the vicinity, but they were trained on the Russian Embassy itself and were therefore of little value. The cameras had, however, caught the actual murder of Laila Daudova on film and had captured some quality pictures of her co-demonstrators.

Officers were dispatched to try to find out what they could about the suspected weapon and where it might have been obtained, and to double-check Laila's financial and phone records. Efforts would be made to confirm or disprove Rasul Daudov's alibi that he was working at the parking lot at the time of the shooting. Timelines outlining the movements of everyone with a connection to the case were being developed.

Liz had a few more questions for the Russians, and she and Ouellette planned to meet the other Chechen demonstrators, as well as the people from the activist group known as Independence United.

Apart from her husband, Rasul, the only person who seemed to have known Laila relatively well was an elderly woman whose granddaughter had disappeared during the Chechen wars, and who joined in the small demonstration whenever her health permitted. Laila, according to Rasul, had been particularly friendly with Mrs. Umarova. She had been suspicious and evasive when first interviewed, but she was also clearly horrified by Laila's death. Mrs. Umarova had initially been interviewed by uniform, but Liz and Ouellette thought she might be worth speaking with in greater depth.

Mrs. Umarova lived in a small apartment above a Chinese grocery in the west end of Ottawa. The apartment was sparsely furnished, and Liz found herself wondering how the woman had managed to afford even these few sticks of furniture. The photographs covering the available surfaces soon led to the answer: the young man in the photos was Mrs. Umarova's son, who had managed to bring her to Canada and was supporting her after a fashion. There were other photographs, many of a lovely young woman in traditional dress. This was the missing granddaughter, whom the old woman refused to let disappear forever.

"Did you know Laila well?" asked Liz, after settling into an uncomfortable wooden chair. It was evidently the best the hostess could offer. She and Ouellette had been presented tea with some ceremony.

"Not well," said Mrs. Umarova haltingly. "Good girl. Loved her little brother. Why she killed? Who? Not idea." Her tiny frame shuddered briefly.

Ouellette gazed around the tiny apartment, impressed that such an elderly, frail woman with poor language skills was surviving at all so far away from her homeland. Apart from the family photos, no decoration was evident. The kitchen, bedroom, and living room were all one space and the bathroom, concluded Ouellette, was behind the only door. A smell of boiled cabbage permeated the room.

"Did you see her, apart from the demonstrations?" asked Liz.

"Sometime. Yes. She come for tea." Mrs. Umarova looked up at Liz and added, "She sad."

"Sad? Because of her brother?"

"Yes, brother. Husband too." Mrs. Umarova halted and gazed into her chipped cup.

"Her husband?"

"Yes," assented Mrs. Umarova, with the air of someone who had just given up. "Yes. He, Daudov, a good man, but very—what word—traditional." Looking up quickly, she added by way of apology, "Traditional, very good. Very good. Yes." She went back to staring into her cup.

"Perhaps, too traditional?"

"No, normal," said Mrs. Umarova vaguely, "but worried about Laila. Wants her to stay home. Hates demonstrations. Tried to stop her to go. Afraid of Russians."

"But she insisted on going to the demonstrations?"

The old woman nodded. "She loved brother. Could not understand why he did not come with them, when they went away from Grozny. He never came to join them, as they plan. She blamed Russians. Me too," she said, glancing towards one of the photographs of her granddaughter.

Mrs. Umarova's face was deeply lined and her grey hair very thin. She appeared to be tiring quickly. Still, Liz found herself wondering if this woman was as old as she looked. She might have been decades younger but was worn by fear and war and tragedy.

Liz didn't want to ask the question, but went on.

"Do you think that Laila's husband might have been capable of killing his wife?"

"Capable," said Mrs. Umarova slowly. "Capable. You mean able? Able—mmm—perhaps." She gave a small shrug. "Laila was unhappy. She loved husband, but they argue about demonstrations. Every day, some time. She was good girl. Very good girl." Liz saw the tears starting in her eyes.

"You do not know how it is to start again in new country," said Mrs. Umarova abruptly. "So hard." Liz and Ouellette nodded in unison. "Old ways, new ways. Old language, new language. How to behave. What to say. Who to trust," she said with a quick look at Liz. "But capable, you ask," said the old woman, returning to the question. "Of course, capable." Then she added with another shrug, "Everybody capable."

"Did you know the other protestors at all?" asked Ouellette.

The old woman peered into the young sergeant's face for a moment, then said, "Not much. Some Canadians from protest group. Don't know why they there. Never visited Chechnya, they said. And young woman with husband missing—never talked to her. Knew a bit a young man with twin brother. Brother taken by Russians too."

Mrs. Umarova didn't provide any further information, but she did have the name of an apartment building in Hull where the young man, Glausov, was living. Liz wondered how the old woman knew this, but in answer to the question, Mrs. Umarova said that the small Chechen community kept in occasional contact. "For security," she said knowingly. Liz thought that the woman was probably paranoid, doubtless about the Russians. Or was Liz being naïve?

Liz and Ouellette left the woman to the rest of her day, whatever that would comprise. The interview had left both of them depressed.

Liz and Ouellette crossed the Champlain Bridge in search of the apartment building in Hull where Glausov lived. Les Sables was a derelict three-storey walk-up in a seedy part of town. The staircase was in such bad shape that, on ascending, Ouellette found himself wondering why the building hadn't been condemned years ago.

The studio apartment rented by Omar Glausov was cramped and cold. It reeked of tobacco smoke, and the smell was unpleasant, even to a confirmed smoker like Liz. He allowed them into the apartment, regarding them with deep suspicion from under a heavy brow. He gestured to them to sit down and they complied, squashed together on a stained sofa that sagged heavily in the middle.

Glausov sat on the edge of a wooden chair that appeared equally uncomfortable. Apart from a small table that Liz could see in the kitchen, this appeared to be the sum total of his furnishings. She concluded that Glausov must sleep on this two-seat plaid sofa. *Was this*, she wondered, *what he had imagined as a better life than the one he'd left behind in Grozny?* A small carpet was rolled up in a corner—*perhaps a prayer rug*, thought Liz—and an eight-by-twelve black-and-white photograph, seemingly of Omar himself, was propped up against Glausov's chair.

Omar Glausov followed Liz's gaze.

"Is brother. Ayub. Is . . . mmm . . ." He was searching for a word and found it. "Jumeau."

"Twin," said Ouellette quickly. Glausov nodded. "Twin. I confuse sometimes, French, English." He shrugged his shoulders. Liz knew how he felt.

Ouellette was watching the man closely and jotting down notes, but mostly he was trying to keep his shoulder from pressing too hard against his boss. She felt equally awkward, trying not to lean too far into her sergeant's side. The only way to get remotely comfortable on the saggy sofa would have been to rest against each other, but neither of them wanted to do that, so each struggled to keep their balance and their dignity.

Glausov did not appear to notice their discomfort. "Ayub disappeared three years. We should meet in Yerevan then go to West. He never come to Yerevan. Finally I must leave, without him. Russians got him. Yes." He nodded heavily as he spoke the last word, and lit a short cigarette.

Ouellette, intrigued by the various illegal routes apparently used by individuals and families to flee the troubles in their own countries, vowed to find Yerevan on a map as soon as they returned to the office.

"How well did you know Laila Daudova?" he asked.

"Yes," answered Glausov.

After a short pause Liz said, "Yes, but did you know her well?"

"No." He shook his head sadly.

Further questioning elicited little. Glausov worked as a janitor at a local mosque, was unmarried, and had family back in Chechnya. There seemed to have been a vague plan for the parents to join the twin brothers in Canada once they had become established. Glausov had no idea where the other protestor, the young widow, lived. And no, he could not think of anyone who would want to hurt Laila Daudova. Except, of course, the Russians.

Liz and Ouellette freed themselves inelegantly from the sofa and thanked Glausov for his time. On their way back to the car, Liz found herself feeling a bit sorry for the Russians, who seemed to be accused as a matter of course. Which wasn't to say their hands were clean, but it was starting to sound as though "Russians" were to blame for a great deal.

"How should we get the address of this other woman, the widow, who was protesting outside the embassy?"

Suddenly Liz realized that the Russian Embassy probably held all that information, and a great deal more. There were, in fact, a few things she would like to discuss with the embassy, though she was disheartened to realize that she would probably have to make a formal request through Foreign Affairs.

Stanislav Mikhailovich Ivanov, cultural attaché of the Russian Embassy in Ottawa, was staring out his window onto Charlotte Street at the spot where Laila Daudova had fallen to a gunshot two days earlier. He remembered with a wry smile that the ambassador had made a comment about him looking out the window at the time, not working, when they had spoken with the RCMP woman.

Ivanov was enough of a veteran not to take his ambassador too seriously. At forty-four, Ivanov had had a long career in the diplomatic, and other, services. Unlike some of his colleagues, he had seamlessly and professionally navigated the upheavals occasioned by the collapse of the Soviet Union. He was good at his job and was not about to be fired just because Ambassador Krasnikov might think him a slacker.

Typically, Ivanov ignored his ambassador as much as possible. At the moment, though, he shared Krasnikov's concern that the murder could have serious consequences for Russia-Canada relations. The ambassador had been on the phone with Moscow several times a day since the assassination, providing updates on his discussions with Foreign Affairs and briefings on how the matter was being treated by the press.

Ivanov had thought Laila Daudova very attractive, when he took time to observe the demonstrators—despite her being a Chechen. Lovely skin, eyes almost black. He had seen her smile once or twice. But she was nowhere near as beautiful as the blue-eyed, raven-haired Madina Grigoryeva. Madina was in a class all her own, according to Ivanov, who considered himself something of an expert on female comeliness.

Ivanov wondered when the demonstrators would turn up again. There had been no sign of them since the murder. Not even the Independence United crowd had put in an appearance. Now *those* people were a mystery to Ivanov. He doubted that any of them could find Grozny on a map, let alone understand what was going on there.

He lit a cigarette, his thoughts flitting to the RCMP woman who was investigating the killing. He recalled that she had turned rather an odd colour when she took her first draw from the Russian cigarette he proffered. He had since learned, among other things, that Inspector Liz Forsyth, of Aylmer, Quebec, was divorced and childless, and had recently returned from England where she had investigated that fascinating murder at the Canadian High Commission.

Ivanov had read with great interest the reports on that case. The murder of a Canadian diplomat within the Canadian High Commission itself had been sensational. Ambassador Krasnikov had convened a special meeting to discuss the incident and how best to respond. In the end, it was decided that the ambassador would send a letter of condolence to the Canadian Foreign Affairs Minister.

Ivanov wondered whether he should make contact with RCMP Inspector Forsyth. Doubtless some of the Chechens had already suggested that the Russians were behind the shooting. Perhaps this would be a good time to make nice and to explain a bit about the situation in the motherland. More importantly, he needed to know how the investigation was proceeding. He put out his cigarette and riffled through some papers. He knew he had her phone number somewhere.

SEVEN
England

Detective Chief Inspector Hay was reviewing, yet again, the files on the Sophie Bouchard killing. Slumped over his desk, he leafed through reports and notes as daylight ebbed away and darkness crept across the London streets. This case was gnawing at him, not least because of his impression of the dead girl's mother, Marie. She and her only daughter had been very close. Mme Marie Bouchard had known from the outset that something was wrong when she lost contact with Sophie after Christmas.

Of course Marie Bouchard had been devastated. There was something in her reaction to her daughter's death that had touched Stephen Hay deeply. Some desperation, some loss of hope. Her own future had been obliterated along with that of her daughter. Mme Bouchard had been virtually silent when Hay accompanied her to the airport for her return flight. The High Commission had assisted in organizing the transport of Sophie's remains back to Montreal, and Acting High Commissioner Rochon, along with Consular Chief Angela Mortenssen, were also in attendance.

Just prior to boarding, Marie Bouchard had turned her red, puffy eyes to Hay.

"You must catch this man, Chief Inspector. You must. No one could have hated Sophie. No one. You must find him." With that, she gave her arm to Paul Rochon, who escorted her through the gathering throng of passengers and onward to passport control.

Her grief, her suffering, and her parting words stayed with Hay; he grew increasingly frustrated by the lack of progress on the case and the dearth of any useful evidence. The few items found at the crime scene—the cigarette package, condom, and pop bottle—had been sent for further analysis. Hay, however, very much doubted that anyone who left such a pristine crime scene would be likely to leave any identifying markers on a condom or bottle. The murder had been carefully planned, the killer highly organized.

The amount of Rohypnol, along with the alcohol in the girl's system, would have rendered her almost unconscious—an easy target for suffocation. But the girl had been found lying on her side; surely it would have been easier to smother her from above, with her lying on her back. Or had she been rolled onto her side post mortem? It must have taken a strong person to do that. The few cameras that were working at the estate that night were focused solely on the entrances to the building. They were being scanned for anything suspicious, but nothing had turned up yet.

He looked again at the photo of Sophie that her mother had brought in for identification purposes. A young woman laughing at something funny. He fleetingly wondered what she had been laughing about. Sophie was clearly fleshy, but (Hay tried to save himself from the cliché, but it was too late) she had a pretty face.

Hay knew that, when travelling, people let down their guard. Everything seems new and different to a tourist, so it can be difficult or impossible to tell if something is unusual or even suspicious. Things that would seem odd or out of place at home might be, or at least appear, perfectly normal someplace else. Consequently, travellers could easily become targets. Sophie Bouchard had been far away from family and friends; her idea of what was "normal" might have become a little blurred.

He thought again of the girl's mother. *Poor woman*, he thought for the umpteenth time. He knew that Mme Bouchard was divorced and would have returned to an empty house in Montreal, never to see her beloved daughter again. *Damn*, he thought, *I must be missing something*. He swallowed some remnants of cold, black coffee and lit a cigarette—the office was virtually empty anyway—and went back to the beginning of the file.

It wasn't just DCI Hay who was frustrated by the lack of progress on the Bouchard case. Detective Sergeant Richard

Wilkins was similarly preoccupied. Wilkins found it difficult to imagine that not a single person in the Mallard Council Estate had seen or heard anything unusual on the night of the murder.

He had spent a considerable amount of time reviewing the interview reports from the estate, and concluded that at least a couple of Mallard's denizens should be interviewed again. One middle-aged woman had reported that she "might have seen" someone hanging about that evening but could give no particulars; a young mother initially told the police that she had heard what sounded like a struggle but later retracted her story.

The charming Gemma, however, was becoming annoyed. Across from her sat Richard Wilkins, her beloved, in one of the trendiest new restaurants in the neighbourhood. It was her birthday. And he had given her a very odd and somewhat unpleasant oil painting as a birthday present.

She might as well have been at home in front of the television for all the attention he was paying her. He had that all-too-familiar look on his face. She studied his face, although she knew this look intimately. Forehead creased, small frown lines between his brows, jaw taut and working. Gemma had the impression that his eyes were somehow staring backwards, gazing at an object in the back of his head rather than anything in actual view. Like, for instance, her. She had taken especial care with her appearance tonight. Not that she didn't do so every time she went out—she joked to friends that she put on make up to take out the garbage—but she had made a real effort this evening. She looked pretty good, too, she thought. The waiter, at least, seemed to think so, smiling at her roguishly as he poured the Pinot Grigio.

Gemma's long, fair hair was secured at the crown, and loopy curls tumbled down her back. She was wearing a fitted dress with a pale blue background and a floral motif in teal and emerald. Her thus-far silent escort was wearing his navy sport coat and grey flannel trousers. *If only he weren't so damned good-looking*, thought Gemma, taking a sip of her wine. *Balding a bit, perhaps, but very handsome. And very intelligent. And*, she sighed, *witty*. Although she could have done without his dreadful puns.

"Richard," she said. And then again, "Richard?"

The young man roused himself, focused at least one of his eyes, and said, "Yes, darling, what is it?"

"You're doing it again."

"Doing what again?"

"Ignoring me. Thinking about work, no doubt."

"I'm sorry," he said guiltily. "And on your birthday, too. I really am sorry. It's just this case . . ."

"It's always some case or another," said Gemma peevishly. "Can't you just let it go for the evening? It's not like she's going anywhere." Of course she immediately regretted having said that. Richard was looking at her with something very much like horror.

"No, she's not," replied Wilkins steadily, "and not likely to either."

"I'm sorry," she said, and meant it. "It's just that sometimes we don't seem to . . . connect, I guess, anymore."

"I'm sorry," he said, realizing as he said it that, these days, they seemed to do nothing but apologize to each other.

The beaming waiter sidled up to the table, flourishing a small pad and pen. They placed their orders—everything on the menu seemed to be "Asian-inspired"—and looked around the restaurant. It was lively—clearly the newest place to see and be seen—and the music was too loud. Having had this thought, Wilkins wondered if he wasn't becoming like his DCI, Hay, who typically preferred more sedate establishments. Shuddering at the thought of suddenly turning into his boss, he said to Gemma, "It's been a difficult week. I suspect that Hay is still in the office." Of course he would never have called his superior "Hay" within earshot. It would have been "Sir" or perhaps "Guv" or even "Boss," but he felt he could indulge in the use of the surname here.

"I understand," said Gemma, raising her cool blue eyes from the tablecloth. She probably didn't understand, but at least she was making an effort. "I know you can't talk about the case, but from what I've seen in the papers it sounds ghastly. It's just that I sort of, you know, *miss* you sometimes."

Wilkins nodded. He understood perfectly. During training, it was emphasized that police work was hellish on families and loved ones. That the stress of being married to or involved with a police officer could become unbearable. That children could be left damaged, terrified, or severely depressed. And that it took a very special person to withstand that stress and to resist succumbing to the fear that he or she could be widowed at any moment.

Yes, Wilkins understood that well enough. But his ongoing doubt was whether Gemma was, in fact, that "very special person." He loved her. Of that he was sure. She was intelligent, funny, stunning, had a great job in advertising and, as a bonus, her family was moneyed. But Gemma was pretty high-maintenance and he knew that she wanted more of him than he could ever really give. They muddled through, though, and both continually attempted to "work" at the relationship. *Although, do you really need to work at a relationship if it's the right one?* He didn't know the answer to that one.

Wilkins took a long pull on the Pinot and smiled across at Gemma. "So," he said, "sorry" (there was that word again) "but I have been pretty preoccupied. I'll give it a rest. How was your day?"

Gemma, slightly mollified, smiled back and began recounting her day at the office.

DCI Hay sank into his usual booth at the Bull's Head. It was late, but it felt a bit like going home, following a long day that had achieved exactly nothing. At least here he could unwind, if only a little.

Billy Treacher brought Hay his pint of bitter and returned to the bar. Billy wondered what had happened to the petite brunette who had been with Hay once or twice the previous month. She had been quite attractive, and the two of them seemed to get along well. Had some sort of accent, American probably. Oh well, none of his business. He went off to microwave the shepherd's pie Hay had ordered for dinner.

Hay sighed heavily. He picked up his pint and tasted it. It always tasted the same, he thought wryly, unless the pipes were clogged. He sighed once more and wondered, again, what on earth had befallen the young woman behind the estate.

He couldn't stop thinking about the case. Sophie had been drinking—several witnesses had attested to that and it had been confirmed by forensics. No one who had been interviewed at the hostel could say if she was drunk or not, because they had, by all accounts, been bladdered themselves. Then there was the Rohypnol, and the absence of any sort of sexual activity. No signs of violence.

She had been close to her family. Her parents were divorced but, while she lived with her mother, she apparently spent time with her father as well. Sophie's older brother had been devastated to hear of her death, although had apparently remarked to an RCMP officer that she had always been her father's "favourite."

Sophie had never been married. No kids. No known boyfriends. Very few close friends, but the ones she had were devoted to her. Anyway, they had all been in Canada at the time of the murder. Hay found it interesting that she had told her mother she wanted to take a criminology course at a community college in Montreal when she'd finished her travels. *What had she been planning to do with that?* he wondered.

Billy Treacher presented Hay the shepherd's pie. Hay stared at the unnatural, angry steam rising from it, thinking he could have made the same thing at home. He did, in fact, have some of the same product in his freezer. But the beer was a lot better here.

EIGHT

Canada

Liz was to meet the cultural attaché of the Russian Embassy, Stanislav Ivanov, for lunch at a popular, if a bit kitschy, Italian restaurant on Somerset. The venue had been suggested by Ivanov, and Liz briefly wondered if he knew that her favourite type of cuisine was Italian. She had spoken to her Super about Ivanov's unexpected invitation immediately after the phone call, uncertain if such a meeting would be useful or dangerous, professional or undiplomatic. Her Super then spent some time making phone calls. Liz didn't know with whom he was checking and didn't much care to know, but later in the day she had been advised that she could accept Ivanov's invitation, provided she made a full report of the encounter immediately afterward. And she was to make sure that she paid for her own lunch.

She arrived early and was escorted to a small table in a corner, with a narrow window on one side, a red-and-white checked tablecloth, and a small vase of variegated carnations in the middle. Liz couldn't help but feel like she was in a Le Carré thriller, even though the Cold War was, ostensibly, over.

She looked suspiciously at the carnations, half expecting to see a microphone wire trailing from the blooms, then swept her eyes across the room to get a look at her fellow patrons. The feeling of intrigue was heightened as she immediately laid eyes on a balding man scratching his nose. It was none other than Lawrence Fletcher, the CSIS agent she had met some days ago in the Super's office. Fletcher was with a bulky companion in a black suit, whose back was to Liz. The CSIS agent glanced at Liz with a mild expression and no flicker of recognition.

Liz was relieved when the waiter brought her the menu, which afforded her something else to look at. She checked her watch, which registered exactly 12:27. Two minutes later and right on time, the Russian cultural attaché strode into the restaurant. He smiled broadly at Liz and made his way to the table. Liz imagined that he shot a knowing smirk towards Fletcher's table, but she couldn't be sure.

"Good afternoon, Inspector," he said, his even, yellowing teeth glinting behind a smile. "How are you?"

"Very well, thank you," she replied a bit stiffly, trying not to catch Fletcher's eye over Ivanov's right shoulder. "How are you?" He, too, was well. Liz noticed for the first time what a large, evidently fit man Ivanov was. Perhaps during their first meeting he had been dwarfed by the ambassador's personal assistant. Ivanov was wearing a well-cut grey suit with a striped tie. His grey-blonde hair was brushed straight back from his face, accentuating high cheekbones and an angular chin. In sum, he was a good-looking man, and he knew it. *Early forties*, reckoned Liz.

He ordered a bottle of Chianti in flawless Italian—at least so far as Liz could tell it was flawless. The waiter, who smiled at him in recognition and replied in the same language, hustled off to obtain the required beverage.

"So, you're quite the polyglot," said Liz conversationally.

"No," replied Ivanaov. "I never have successfully mastered Hungarian."

Liz was about to smile at the joke, but Ivanov looked quite serious, then told her that the veal here was very good. He was, in fact, a charming lunch companion, and Liz quickly forgot about Fletcher. Ivanov said he was originally from St. Petersburg but had studied in Moscow and joined the diplomatic corps shortly after graduation. And yes, in response to a question from Liz, he had been tutored privately in English by an Englishwoman. That explained the touch of a London accent to his speech.

Liz decided on the chicken piccata, while Ivanov (now insisting incongruously on "Stan") ordered veal saltimbocca. Before lunch arrived, however, Stan asked Liz how the investigation into Laila Daudova's murder was proceeding. She had rehearsed the answer to this question and told him, essentially, as much as she would have told a journalist.

Following leads, speaking to friends and family, trying to get to know more about her, usual police procedure. Did Ivanov—er, Stan—remember seeing anything else from the window on the day she was shot?

He leaned towards her and regarded her with an air of considerable confidentiality. Liz felt quite deflated when he simply told her that he could remember nothing else. He had seen the woman drop to the ground and the blood seeping through her outer clothing. He hadn't heard the shot and, while he had looked quickly across the street, saw nothing and no one on the other side.

She had to ask if any embassy cameras might have picked up the shooter. Ivanov raised his eyebrows.

"No," he replied. "Our cameras are solely for the security of the premises."

Liz quickly dropped the issue. If the embassy didn't want to discuss its security arrangements, or any other type of surveillance, it would do no good to pursue the matter.

"But," he continued, "it is important for you to know something about the Chechens." At that moment, the waiter appeared, bearing two very large white dinner plates, and presented lunch with some ceremony. Perfectly seasoned pasta accompanied both the chicken and the veal, and the aroma of garlic, butter, and thyme rose with the steam. Both meals paired well with the fruity Chianti that Liz had accepted (to be polite, she told herself).

Ivanov raised his glass and said with a broad smile, "*Na zdorovie.*"

Liz raised her glass said something similar back to him, and they began to eat. Glancing up, Liz noticed that Fletcher was having his coffee refilled, although she didn't know how many times he might already have done so.

After a few bites, Ivanov returned to his subject. The Chechens were, according to him, a fractious people who had never appreciated how much they had benefitted from being a part of Russia. They were a mountain-dwelling, lawless people, prone to radicalism and terrorist acts. They blamed Russia for all the troubles in their province, and the accusation that the Russians were responsible for·the disappearances of their loved ones was just the latest in a long line of grievances.

Following a brief history of the region (which, Liz privately acknowledged, largely tallied with the one provided earlier by the indefatigable Sergeant Ouellette), Ivanov said that despite the bad blood between ethnic Russians and Chechens, the Russian Embassy in Canada would have no reason whatsoever to be involved in the assassination of a Chechen Canadian. Liz wasn't certain that she believed this. He had gone on at some length, and Liz was left wondering if he wasn't, perhaps, protesting too much.

The waiter reappeared, smiling, and inclined his head quizzically towards Ivanov. Ivanov nodded, although Liz didn't know to what he was assenting. Presently they were ushered into a small, private smoking room on the second floor. If she wondered whether the Russian would take advantage of their privacy and pass her a brown paper envelope or some sort of bribe, she was mistaken. He merely poured her some espresso and offered a Russian cigarette, which she declined in favour of her own less-noxious brand. *Fletcher*, thought Liz, *must be having kittens.*

Liz asked him casually over coffee if he had any information about the blue-eyed Chechen widow who regularly attended the demonstrations. Stan looked a bit taken aback by the question.

"Why would I know about her?" he asked, then took a long pull on his cigarette.

"I just wondered," answered Liz, watching him closely.

"I think her name is Madina something or other," he said, smoke issuing from his nose.

"Do you think you might have any information about her at the embassy? We haven't been able to track her down."

"Perhaps," he replied.

"It would be very useful," said Liz. "We really want to speak with anyone who knew her."

Ivanov studied her with steady blue eyes. "I will see what I can find."

"And you'll phone me?"

"Yes."

Later that afternoon, when Liz debriefed her Super on the meeting, he burst into laughter upon hearing that Fletcher from csis had been at the restaurant. Ouellette, also in attendance, grinned as well, in part because the Super was so overcome that the front buttons of his uniform looked perilously close to popping off.

Stanislav Ivanov brushed some fine, powdery snow off the shoulders of his overcoat and hung it on the wooden coat rack in the corner of his office. He sat down slowly, feeling a bit uneasy. Ivanov had managed to maintain his professional demeanour and exercise his considerable personal charm during his lunch with Inspector Forsyth. He had worked hard to keep his curiosity about the status of the investigation under control.

He had found it difficult to gauge what the inspector herself had been thinking and where both he and the embassy stood with respect to the investigation. Not that anyone from the embassy could be touched by Canadian authorities—diplomatic immunity protected them from that. It could, however, turn very nasty indeed if anyone from the embassy was implicated in the murder. Moscow would be furious, and the political ramifications could be dire—not just in Canada, but in more important countries as well.

His ambassador had agreed that a lunch with Forsyth would be a good idea, to give her a bit of perspective about Chechnya and to try to find out where the investigation stood. He had succeeded, he thought, with the former objective but failed on the second.

At least the murder of Laila Daudova had achieved one desirable outcome: not a single demonstration had taken place outside the embassy since her death. Sadly, as a result, he could no longer watch the beautiful, blue-eyed Madina Grigoryeva from his window. He quite missed that.

He summoned his secretary, gave her Madina's full name and address, and told her to provide the information to Inspector Liz Forsyth of the Royal Canadian Mounted Police.

Liz drove back to Aylmer, through the dark Ottawa streets and across the Champlain Bridge to the Quebec side. It was snowing, and a heavy snowfall was expected overnight. The blowing snow and darkness, broken only by the juddering reflection of oncoming headlights, would have seemed eerie were it not so commonplace. Liz had to collect Rochester from her neighbours, the Greens. She was exhausted.

She knew that she shouldn't have a dog, with her heavy work schedule and great reliance upon her neighbours to look after him during her many absences. But nobody had told Rochester that Liz shouldn't have a dog. He had lolloped into her yard one day and might as well have announced that he was adopting her. She checked with the SPCA and placed ads in the local papers, but no one came forward to claim him.

Without a collar or tags, his provenance was unknown, as was his breeding. She talked to the Greens before making things official. They urged her to keep the dog and offered their services to look after him any time. Privately, they thought that she could use the company. Nice girl like that, working all hours and living by herself. Poor thing could use a companion, and a dog would be just the thing.

The Greens had a point, although Liz would have been mortified to hear herself described as a "poor thing." Rochester was, however, great company. He certainly tried his best to wag away Liz's stress and ward off the depression that sometimes overtook her when dealing with especially disturbing cases.

He was big and black and hairy, and she had called him Rochester while going through a Brontë phase. She still preferred reading the classics to more modern literature, and she abhorred crime fiction. Too much like work. Work.

Laila Daudova. Another interview tomorrow. As she had suspected, Ivanov had been able to provide her the name and address of the lovely demonstrator who had lost her husband to, the young widow believed, the Russians.

The forecast had been correct and a good deal of snow had fallen during the night. Liz went out to warm up the engine and brush the snow off the Honda, wishing for the umpteenth time that she had rented a house with a garage. Given the amount of fluffy snow on the car's roof, some ten inches of the stuff had fallen. She was relieved that the snowplough had already made it through her neighbourhood, although she realized that she could have problems manoeuvring her car over the pile of snow now deposited at the end of the driveway.

She had come back inside to pick up her purse, briefcase, and dog when the phone rang. It was Hay. The snow on her boots was already melting into dirty puddles on the kitchen floor and her coat felt damp and heavy.

"This time difference is quite awkward, isn't it?" Hay remarked after the initial pleasantries.

"Yes," she replied, dragging a nearby kitchen chair towards the back doorway and sinking into it. "Five hours is really inconvenient."

"Oh," he said hastily, "if it's a bad time—"

"No, no," she interjected, realizing how she had sounded. *Off to another brilliant start*, she thought. "Actually, your timing is good. Just getting ready to go to the office."

"Oh, alright then. Good. I'm working at home at the moment and thought I'd give you a ring."

"Good," said Liz. Then she plunged on bravely. "It's good to hear your voice."

"And yours."

Okay, now what? she thought. There was an uncomfortable silence, then suddenly they both began talking at once, asking each other about the headway, or lack thereof, they were making on their respective cases. Once they sorted out who would speak first, they settled into a reasonable sort of dialogue and eventually relaxed into conversation.

Liz was interested to learn that Hay had spent a couple of evenings at cultural events hosted for visiting Canadian artists by the High Commission. He seemed to enjoy the company of Paul Rochon, the Acting High Commissioner, through whom he had met a painter, a poet, and an eclectic assortment of "wannabe" artists. Hay and Wilkins would be attending a performance of a Canadian jazz dance company later in the week.

No, Liz had not heard of Louise Chapman, the painter from Saskatchewan, nor did she know of a poet from Burlington. As to the latter, Hay told Liz that she wasn't missing much, but he had been very impressed by Chapman's work. Liz was starting to feel she was lacking in some degree of culture—*Canadian* culture, no less—but was somewhat cheered that she recognized the name of the jazz dance company.

"I wouldn't normally go to these things," said Hay. "But they make a break from trying to figure out who killed that poor young girl. As I've told you, we have very little to go on. It's good of Rochon to include us in the invitations. And," he continued, "since you Canadians seem bent on getting into trouble over here, it's probably just as well that I keep up my diplomatic connections."

Liz smiled, then briefly wondered to whom "us" referred.

Hay expressed concern about the aftermath of the ice storm, as he was still hearing news reports of storm damage and power outages, but Liz reassured him that, in Aylmer and Ottawa at least, things were pretty much back to normal. Large parts of the province of Quebec, however, were still suffering badly.

Hay then asked after Rochester's health, which unaccountably pleased Liz. "Well, I'd better get going," she said, having assured Hay that Rochester was well. "I have to drop him off at the neighbours and then meet Ouellette for another witness interview. Thanks so much for calling."

"Very nice to talk to you, too," he said. And then, since he didn't know what else to say, he said goodbye.

NINE
England

Acting Canadian High Commissioner Paul Rochon said goodbye and hung up the phone. The Prime Minister's Office—PMO. Again. Did they actually think the High Commission, in general, and Paul, in particular, were in any way equipped, or even authorized, to solve the Bouchard murder? Paul slumped back into his chair. He found himself craving a cigarette, even though he'd quit almost ten years ago. He wished, yet again, that a replacement for High Commissioner Carruthers would be found quickly.

One of Paul's numerous problems was that the Bouchard case had been widely, and sensationally, reported back in

Canada. Television and print correspondents were on the ground in London at the moment, breathlessly reporting to their Canadian audiences the latest information—or speculation—about the case. Some of the Canadian correspondents had apparently befriended members of the British tabloid press. Each vied with the other to produce the most sensational headlines.

What was, in essence, the tragic end to the life of a young Canadian traveller had somehow become a political football back in Ottawa. Of course, Paul reflected, Canadians died abroad. Happened all the time. But rarely were they murdered and left naked behind council estates. The demanding and frankly irritating PMO official seemed to be calling the High Commission hourly. The PMO was trying hard to keep ahead of the press, but there was little new that Paul could offer.

As for the Canadian foreign minister, he was a harried-looking man at the best of times, and this was certainly not the best of times. Clearly the minister's political staff were doing their best to keep their cerebral but somewhat fragile minister in the loop.

Somehow the Bouchard murder had morphed into a controversy in Canada about government funding for its missions abroad. Rochon found this a puzzling leap. No amount of government funding would have kept Sophie Bouchard alive. The Official Opposition, however, had pounced on the case to demonstrate that Foreign Affairs had been gutted and left virtually without resources, while the second opposition party was claiming that Canadian embassies and High Commissions spent far too much time on official entertaining and hobnobbing with dignitaries, while doing little to protect the interests of Canadians abroad.

Of course, none of this had anything to do with Sophie Bouchard and whoever had taken her life. But it meant that part of Paul's long days now included drafting talking points, responses for Question Period in the House of Commons, and briefing notes for the press. The murder had become a political lightning rod for the ongoing and contentious debate over government funding.

This was taking a toll on Paul Rochon. A nervous man at the best of times, he had virtually lost his appetite and found himself dreading going to the office in the mornings. Worse yet was having to field phone calls from Ottawa in the middle of the night.

Another complication, closer to home, was that no replacement for the murdered Head of the Trade Section, Natalie Guévin, had yet been named. Natalie had been a fine, dedicated officer and Paul missed her calm and professional demeanour. So now the Acting Head of Trade at the High Commission was the arrogant, ambitious Maxwell Shaunessy, the number two in the section.

Paul had had little to do with Shaunessy prior to Natalie's shocking murder. He remembered that Natalie had not been impressed with young Maxwell and hadn't trusted him. *With reason, too*, reflected Paul. He had concluded that Shaunessy was one of those people whose ambition outstripped his talent, so the handsome young officer made up for that deficiency by stealing the contacts of his colleagues and, to coin a phrase, kissing up and kicking down. These tactics, cleverly executed, had resulted in his rapid rise through the ranks.

The rest of the trade section, conscientious and devoted Canadian and local officials, resented and disliked their Acting Head. But there was nothing that Paul could do until Natalie was replaced. He added "call Personnel again re: trade replacement" to his already lengthy to-do list. He didn't know how he would make it through another official dinner that very night, at the residence of the eccentric Swedish ambassador.

The details of inter-jurisdictional cooperation with Canada on the Bouchard case had been ironed out early in the investigation, and the Royal Canadian Mounted Police were in regular contact with their British counterparts. The RCMP had followed up with Sophie's family and friends in Montreal, but little of interest had turned up.

Late on the afternoon of January 22, DCI Hay took a phone call at his home from Inspector Allan Ensworth of the Mounties. Today, Ensworth had some surprising information. During routine investigation into the whereabouts of those close to Sophie, it had come to light that her father, René Bouchard, had in fact been in Amsterdam at the time of the murder. M. Bouchard had not offered this information to the police when first questioned.

It was through routine police work that this had come to light. Bouchard had told his employer and landlord of his planned trip to Amsterdam, and the police subsequently took a good look at the relevant airline manifests. What this might have to do with the murder was unclear, and perhaps disturbing, and Hay hung up the phone, thinking hard. He remembered that Sophie's mother, Marie, was divorced but that Sophie retained a good relationship with her father. What had he been doing in Amsterdam? Did he even know that his daughter was a short plane ride away?

Next morning, prior to the daily meeting of the murder squad, Hay began the process of obtaining clearance to work with the KLPD, or the Dutch National Police Services Agency. He wanted to get a picture of the movements of Sophie's father while he was in Amsterdam. During the murder squad meeting, Wilkins suggested that he wanted to re-interview at least two of the residents of the Mallard Council Estate. Hay agreed readily, assigning him a uniformed officer to go along. At least, he thought, they had a few leads left to follow. The last thing he wanted was for the morale of the team to start flagging due to lack of progress.

DS Wilkins and Police Constable Etheridge contacted the young mother who had initially reported hearing sounds of a struggle and then retracted her statement. This bit of information was of particular interest to Wilkins, because, according to Forensics, there had been no struggle at all during the murder of Sophie Bouchard.

Wilkins rang the bell and a baby began crying immediately. So immediately, in fact, that he briefly wondered if it was something like one of those doorbells that sounded like dogs barking. But no, there was a real baby alright, slung over his mother's hip and bellowing loudly. The child's mother did not appear impressed by her visitors. In fact, she looked as though she hadn't slept for several days. Greasy brown hair hung about her shoulders and there was a purplish hue underneath her eyes.

She waved them in vaguely with her free hand and made

no attempt to quiet the child. Perhaps she had deemed it a lost cause. She placed him in a cot and asked the two young men what they wanted.

"I've already spoken t'your lot," she said, showing bad teeth as she began to speak. "I've nowt else to say."

"Might I ask you, then, what you heard on the night of January 4?" he asked.

"Nowt."

"But initially you thought you did?" He found himself having to speak quite loudly due to the constant wailing of the child.

"I were mistaken."

"About what?"

The young woman looked suspiciously at Wilkins from beneath unkempt brows.

"I thought I 'eard summat, right? I wanted to be 'elpful. I thought as I 'eard some sort o' fight. But there's always fights goin' on 'round 'ere. Any road, t'baby were cryin'." Wilkins glanced over at the cot. The baby's furious little face was florid, his tiny fists clenched in outrage. He kept up a continuous howl, occasionally stopping for breath.

Wilkins soon realized that he wasn't about to learn much here. If the young woman had heard anything, she wasn't about to tell them. And if, in fact, the baby boy had been crying that night, it was even doubtful that any of the neighbours could have heard much. The young PC had reached much the same conclusion and closed his notepad. He felt a migraine coming on.

They said their goodbyes, and, as they were leaving, she said, "You might want try Mrs. Trotter in 345. She told me she'd seen someone 'anging about that night. She's a good 'un, Mrs. Trotter. You could try 'er."

Mrs. Trotter was, in fact, the other person they had on their follow-up list for the Mallard Council Estate. They trudged up to apartment 345, having found the elevator broken. Eileen Trotter was a middle-aged woman living alone. She invited Wilkins and Etheridge into her small, neat flat and, insisting that the kettle had just boiled, quickly produced tea and digestive biscuits.

She's a nice-looking woman, thought Wilkins. *Comfortable, a bit motherly.* A quick look around the flat showed no evidence of children. No photographs, anyway.

"So," she said, "I suppose you're 'ere about the man I saw 'anging about."

"Yes," assented Wilkins. "Can you remember what you saw on January 4th that interested you?"

"Well, it was about four o'clock—"

"Four o'clock," interrupted Wilkins. "As early as that?"

She nodded. "Yeah, it was about four because I was starting to make my dinner. I'd only finished chopping the veg for the spaghetti sauce and the whole works has to simmer for about an hour and a half. I glanced out window."

"Your kitchen window faces . . ."

"North. Towards what some of 'em call a park." Wilkins made a mental note to have a look out the window before they left.

"And what did you see then?"

"A man. Young. By 'is movement, anyways. Bit stringy. Black baseball cap on. Couldn't see 'is face. Jeans and a black overcoat with some markings on back." No, she didn't know what the markings were—maybe a logo or some writing, but nothing she could recognize. "I think 'e 'ad one of them 'oodie things on because it seemed to have come out the back of his coat at the neck."

Not the best description Wilkins had ever heard, but it was all they had so far.

"What interested you?"

"Well, just as I 'adn't seen 'im before. And 'e was moving strange. Going back and forth across path. Almost like 'e was measuring something. Zig-zagging, like."

"How long was he there?"

"I don't know. I wasn't that interested at the time. I put metal screen over t'sauce. To stop it bubbling over," she said, in reply to a curious look from the PC, "and went to watch telly. I s'pose I looked at 'im for a moment. I didn't know it would be important."

Of course she didn't, thought Etheridge, scribbling his notes. *She was making dinner and saw someone outside— hardly reason to call 999.*

"And you didn't recognize him?"

"Nah."

"Have you seen him since?"

"Nah."

"And you're absolutely certain about the time?"

"Yeah. Oh," she said, cocking her head, "I understand. The murder were meant to be committed during the night, weren't it? But no, I saw that man about four o'clock."

Mrs. Trotter was very happy to show off her gleaming kitchen. It was evident to Wilkins that Sophie Bouchard's murder would have been in clear view from the window.

"The little park there—is it floodlit?" he asked.

"It's s'posed to be," agreed Mrs. Trotter, "but lamps been burnt out for ages. Some of us 'uv complained, but . . ." She shrugged.

"Thank you very much for your cooperation. You've been very helpful. And for the tea." Etheridge nodded his appreciation as well, and they left the quiet flat to climb down the drab, concrete stairwell.

"So," said Etheridge, "someone might have planned the attack and was doing a reccy?"

"It's possible," said Wilkins, "although what Sophie Bouchard had to do with this place is anybody's guess. I'll talk to Hay, but I think we should get some of the boys back over here to see if anyone matches the description she gave us. It might not be a bad idea to float the description around Sophie's hostel, either."

In Hay's experience, the Dutch police were extremely efficient, and his latest contact was no exception. Hay learned that Sophie's father, René Bouchard, left Montreal on Thursday, December 25, direct to Amsterdam on a KLM flight. He returned to Canada on Monday, January 6. Bouchard had stayed in Amsterdam for the duration and taken a room in a mid-range hotel. Hay remembered that he, himself, had stayed with that same hotel chain many years ago during a visit to the Netherlands. Cozy, he recalled, with an enormous buffet breakfast. There was no indication that Bouchard had travelled outside Holland during that period. As to his activities in the country, the KLPD hadn't had any reason to monitor the movements of a Canadian tourist.

Why, he wondered, would Bouchard have been travelling on Christmas Day? Granted, it wasn't necessarily a bad decision if you weren't too keen on Christmas. The aircraft would have been almost empty. The return date, too, would have avoided much of the post–New Year rush. So perhaps he was just a canny traveller.

He decided to pass this information on to the RCMP. They could figure out if they wanted to follow up any further with René Bouchard.

"You're joking," Wilkins said in considerable surprise. He had returned from the interviews at the Mallard Council Estate and entered his boss's office as Hay was hanging up the phone.

"I most certainly am not," said Hay, a bit impatiently. "That's what Ensworth of the RCMP office in Ottawa just reported. Six years ago, Sophie Bouchard's father, René, was brought in for questioning in Montreal in connection with the abduction and sexual assault of a young girl. Nothing stuck, and no arrest was made. Apparently a twelve-year-old girl was abducted on her way home from school and molested. Not raped, but fondled, and of course the child was frightened out of her wits. She couldn't provide a very good description, but Bouchard was in the area at the time and drove a similar type of vehicle: a blue van. Why is it always a blue van? Bouchard vaguely resembled the description given by the girl. He had an airtight alibi and was let go."

"I think in the States it's always a white van," said Wilkins irrelevantly.

Hay pushed the fingers of both hands into his white hair and leaned back into his chair. This case was becoming increasingly opaque. That it crossed jurisdictions and required the necessary involvement of Interpol made it all the more cumbersome.

"So what if," said Wilkins, "Bouchard is some sort of sexual predator who's never been caught. Do you think he might have gone to Amsterdam for some sort of sexual tourism?"

"I suppose so," said Hay. "That's possible. Although those types usually go to Asia. But what does it have to do with his daughter? Unless, perhaps, he molested her as a girl?"

"I guess that wouldn't be unheard of," agreed Wilkins. Much as he loved his job, getting into this kind of territory made his skin crawl. His boss was becoming increasingly tetchy as well. Wilkins had noticed this was often the case when an investigation dragged on.

"And he was in Europe during the murder," continued Wilkins, "although we have no information suggesting that he ever left the Netherlands prior to his return to Canada. Even if we want to go down this road, what possible motive could he have to murder his own daughter?"

Hay shook his head. "No idea. But we had best continue to look into this. In any event, the RCMP said they would follow up."

The mood in the office had become sombre. So Wilkins offered, "Or, Sir, we may just have someone who hates cornflakes."

Hay looked up in some confusion. "Hates cornflakes, Wilkins?"

"Yes, Sir. You know. A cereal killer."

"Out, Wilkins," said Hay, pointing towards the door.

"Yes, Sir," said Wilkins as he rose to leave, but they both felt a little less oppressed than they had before.

TEN
Canada

Liz and Ouellette met six members of Independence United at an ill-maintained bungalow in Ottawa's east end. Ouellette privately found the name of the organization to be rather an amusing oxymoron but kept his thoughts to himself. Although the group members had been interviewed previously, Liz was interested to see them for herself.

They were ushered into a small, dingy living room in the basement. It was carpeted throughout with knobbly indoor/outdoor carpeting and furnished with a haphazard assortment of chairs. The room felt chilly; the detectives weren't sure to what extent, if at all, the heat was functioning, so they kept their coats on. Following introductions, Liz and Ouellette were seated on wooden chairs, incongruously covered with frilly, floral seat cushions tied to the slats in the chair-backs. This downstairs apartment, they learned, was rented by one of the young men—Tony Blackwell, an earnest young man sporting a long blonde ponytail and beard.

Liz determined that the six young persons, four men and two women, comprised the entire membership of the Ottawa chapter of Independence United. Tony Blackwell, who had introduced himself as spokesman, launched without preamble into a description of the organization's mandate.

"We believe," he said, regarding Liz sanctimoniously, "that peoples who want to be freed from the government of *any* artificially formed state should have the right to self-determination. We support these efforts everywhere we can."

One of the young women, a stunning red head dressed completely in black and wearing high-heeled black leather boots, added, "Most, if not all, states are artificial. Imposed from outside by elites with their own agendas and no consideration for the people, or the histories and cultures of those they oppress. Just harnessing the people for their own selfish ends, be they political or economic."

Ouellette looked quickly at the faces of the others in the group. They were enraptured. Their faces glowed with the faith of true believers, and all nodded as their Boudicca spoke. While the ponytailed young man was nominally the spokesman, it was clear where the power in this group resided.

"It is down to the individual to decide when and if he, or she, decides to become a part of a larger whole," she continued. "We are all born to be free, to make our own choices, and to decide who we live with. Governments are unnatural and harmful. And of course," she added, "we support many other international causes as well. We stand with any group dedicated to freedom and the resistance of oppression." She raised her chin even higher and fixed her cool blue eyes on Sergeant Gilles Ouellette, as though daring him to disagree with her unimpeachable beliefs.

For his part, Ouellette was itching to enter into a political debate with these imbeciles and demolish their puerile arguments, but held his tongue and continued his note-taking. He couldn't quite fathom whether this group thought they were some sort of anarchists or believed themselves to have invented a novel strain of political theory. *No wonder*, he thought, *they have only six members*. It was surprising they had that many, although it was clear what, or who, the draw was.

Liz, too, was bemused by the political views being spouted with such certitude. The group members were very young. Liz thought they were in their late teens or very early twenties. Perhaps their ages accounted for the simplicity and intensity of their beliefs. In a way, she envied them their conviction but found it difficult to believe this organization was "international." She asked where they were headquartered.

"Cincinnati," came the unexpected reply. The answer was provided by the red-haired vixen, who had introduced herself as Mila Krasniyeva. It might have been interesting to pursue further the origins of the "movement," but Liz could tell that her sergeant was having some trouble smothering a grin, so she asked quickly, "How many of you were at the demonstration outside the Russian Embassy the day that Laila Daudova was killed?"

"Just three of us," the ponytail answered quickly, studying the carpet. "Me, Pierre, and Andrea." Pierre was Pierre Thibault, and Andrea Cumming was the woman who was, well, not red-haired and beautiful.

"Did you go together?"

"No," said Andrea. "We met up at the embassy. It was difficult to get around due to the ice storm, so we all made our own way there."

"Did you know Laila Daudova well?"

"No," answered Andrea. "Didn't even know her name until we saw the news. We, uh, didn't stick around after she was shot. We thought it might be some kind of nut . . . well, it *was* some kind of nut, right? And we didn't want to stay to get shot at. We all took off."

Ouellette interjected innocently, "So you didn't stay to try to help Mrs. Daudova?"

Now, now, thought Liz, grinning inwardly, *don't try to score points, Sergeant.*

"Well," said Pierre, speaking for the first time, "I really did think she was dead. She looked dead. There was lots of blood. We were scared."

"Of course," said Liz, nodding. "Do any of you remember anything, anything at all that happened before the shooting? Anything you saw, or heard, maybe?"

The three shook their heads.

"Something right afterwards, perhaps?"

No, none of them had seen anything. It had been very cold and they were just trying to keep warm, while supporting the Chechens who had lost their loved ones. Then they had fled.

Liz asked them if they knew any of the Chechen demonstrators well. No, the Chechens seemed to be quite inward, according to Pierre. Andrea added that they didn't seem to understand why the demonstrators from Independence United joined in their demonstrations. A brief discussion ensued, during which the young people agreed that any confusion about their role must have been due to the language barrier.

Later, in the car, Ouellette could bite his tongue no longer. "*Tabernac!* What a bunch of crap is that? These people don't have anything better to do? They know *nothing!* So every person should somehow be his very own state if he wants? Where do people *get* these crackpot ideas?"

"Cincinnati," Liz replied gravely, and they both burst into laughter.

"I'm not sure if that group is just naïve, or if they're hiding something," continued Liz. "The ponytail was looking a bit edgy, but then we often have that effect on people." As Ouellette drove the squad car carefully down the gloomy, frozen streets, she added, "Even their name's a bit of an oxymoron, don't you think?"

Rochester growled deeply, shaking his head furiously. His neck and shoulders were low to the ground, paws outstretched, and hindquarters high in the air. He would never relinquish his fearsome grip on his prey, which, in this case, happened to be a somewhat battered bathroom towel that had seen better days. At the other end of the towel was his mistress, Liz, who was on her knees, laughing as she attempted to pull the towel away from the dog. This was Rochester's favourite game. When he won, as he was routinely allowed to, he would take a victory lap around the living room, then present the towel to Liz so they could enjoy another round.

"Good boy," said Liz. "Well done, buddy, but I need a break."

Rochester stopped in mid-lap and, realizing that the game was over, briefly shook the towel in order to break its neck before tossing it aside and taking a nap.

Liz got up from the floor and collapsed into her couch. She lit a cigarette and gazed fondly at her dog. He was certainly a welcome distraction from her case, which was going nowhere fast. As if that wasn't frustrating enough, the brass in the RCMP, the government, and the press were all over the case. She knew that shouldn't bother her, but it did, and it affected her focus.

Forensics had given her everything they had, which was minimal. While Ballistics had determined the type of weapon used, no record of any recent transactions involving such a weapon had turned up. Laila seemed to have had few friends, if any, and the people she *did* know had been demonstrating alongside her. The Chechens were united in blaming the Russians. But why would the Russian Embassy need to kill a young woman involved in tiny, if perhaps annoying, demonstrations?

She leaned back and took a long drag. *What* had *happened to the people who had disappeared in Chechnya?* she wondered. Where was Laila's brother? Dead, or mouldering in a prison somewhere? People disappeared all the time, in every country and for countless reasons. Some had accidents, were murdered, kidnapped, lost their memories, wandered off, left their spouses, assumed new identities. There were numerous reasons why people disappeared. According to the demonstrators, these particular disappearances were political. According to the Russians, it was the Chechen authorities themselves who were responsible.

Rochester opened an eye and, satisfied that Liz was still there, went back to sleep. Liz looked at him through red-rimmed eyes and wished she could do the same.

Maybe, thought Liz, *the answer is closer to home.* Laila's husband had a pretty flimsy alibi. She would get Ouellette to call on Pickwick's Parking, the company that owned several lots in Ottawa, including the one in which Daudov worked. Pickwick's had told police that Daudov signed in at 8:53 on the morning of the day his wife was murdered, and closed the lot more than an hour early—at 5:20—upon learning of his wife's death from one of her fellow demonstrators. They still had no idea of Daudov's movements between those times. Perhaps the company could furnish some additional information.

In fact, Daudov had been told that his wife was dead by the blue-eyed young woman who regularly demonstrated outside the embassy, protesting the disappearance of her husband. The young woman's whereabouts had been unknown until Stanislav Ivanov of the Russian Embassy—or at least his secretary—had provided Liz with her address. Liz and Ouellette were meeting the young woman, Madina Grigoryeva, later in the morning. And Liz thought that another call on Mr. Daudov would also be in order.

Rasul Daudov sat at the small wooden table and was trying to finish a piece of stale toast. Before him were a mug of instant coffee and a picture of his wife, Laila. He hadn't even noticed that large tears were leaking from his eyes onto the plate.

He still couldn't believe that she was gone. This lovely, generous woman who had joyfully fled Chechnya with him, who had consented to be his wife when he had nothing to offer her but vague hopes. *Laila*, he thought. *No, not this. Not my Laila.* He picked up the photo and ran a finger across her face, her lips, somehow hoping it would bring her back.

He hoped and prayed that the Canadian authorities would find the killer. He placed the photo back on the table. Rasul didn't even care that the police evidently suspected him. He hoped they were just being thorough and would soon capture his wife's murderer. But in his heart he knew who the killers were. He knew that the Russians were behind this. In a flash of anger, he glared at her photo, asking himself again why she insisted on going to the demonstrations. *Like a red flag to a bull*, he thought.

Rasul's anger extended itself to Bula, Laila's missing brother, whose disappearance had fuelled Laila's repeated attendance at the demonstrations. He picked up the stained yellow mug and took a last swig of very sweet coffee. *Laila used to tease him about how much sugar he took*, he thought sadly. *Bad for his health.*

Today he would go to the parking lot on Montreal Road. That was his job, and anyway, he had nothing else to do. A couple of days earlier he had been building a new life for himself and Laila. Now the future looked black, frightening, and lonely. Rasul heaved a sigh and pushed himself back from the table. Slowly he put on his heavy boots and thrift store parka, and walked mechanically down the stairs to the entrance of the apartment building.

The bus stop was a few moments' walk from the building, but the sidewalk was icy and a stiff wind was blowing from the north. He paused to pull the hood of his parka over his head.

Suddenly he felt himself carried upward and back by an unseen force. As he hit the concrete, the blast of excruciating pain kicked in and he could no longer breathe. The pain didn't last for long, though. He gave one mighty twitch. And, in an instant, Rasul Daudov lay dead on the Ottawa sidewalk, his dark eyes still wide with shock, his blood soaking through his thrift store parka.

The telephone rang as Andrea Cumming was attempting to pull a comb through her wet, tangled hair. Andrea, the other female member of the Ottawa chapter of Independence United, was not a great beauty like her associate Mila Krasniyeva and, no matter how short she cut it or how long she wore it, her fine, frizzy hair engaged her in daily confrontation. Andrea was getting ready to go to her part-time cashier job at Zellers. She was surprised to hear the phone ringing so early.

"Hello?" she said, her wet feet sticking to the linoleum floor in the kitchen.

"Andrea. It's Tony." It was Tony Blackwell, her ponytailed confederate from Independence.

"Tony, hi. What's up?"

"I just wanted to make sure that you—well, I'm sure you wouldn't—but just wanted to make sure that you won't say anything about, well, the demonstration the day that woman was killed."

"I told you," said Andrea, frowning. "You know you can count on me."

"I do, I do know," said Tony hurriedly. "It's just that, you know, this is, well, different." Blackwell's palms were sweating and the handset of his phone was becoming sticky.

"Yes, Tony. And I know you don't want to let Mila down," she said, with just a trace of bitterness in her voice.

"Thanks so much, Andrea. I owe you one."

"No problem. I have to go now. I have to get to work."

"Okay, thanks again. See you soon."

Andrea hung up the phone, unstuck her feet from the floor, and resumed battling her hair.

Liz and Ouellette were among the first at the crime scene, although it was already cordoned off and uniformed officers were keeping curious passersby at a distance. The murdered Daudov lay flat on his back, blood pooling around his torso. He had almost been smashed into the front of the apartment building by the force of the bullet. His dark eyes were wide open and his face frozen in shock. He had clearly been hit square in the chest and appeared to have died instantly.

The coroner and forensics teams arrived and carried out their duties quietly and professionally. Photos were taken, as were measurements, while police attempted to track down eyewitnesses. A couple of people who had come down from the apartment building had seen the shooting, if not the shooter, and were giving statements.

It didn't take an expert in forensics to determine the cause of death, although Liz was trained not to reach conclusions prior to having all relevant information. But she had seen a similar crime scene very recently.

Who, she wondered, *could have wanted both the Daudovs dead? Who would have wanted to cut short their attempt to make a new life?* Liz and Ouellette rode back in silence to an emergency meeting of the task force, each mentally pursuing various scenarios that rapidly hit dead ends.

A grim group of officers convened that afternoon in their cramped headquarters. The meeting had been struck as soon as the crime scene had been processed and the bloody corpse of Rasul Daudov transported to the morgue.

Maps and photos of the Russian Embassy, Laila Daudova, and the crime scene on Charlotte Street were attached to the variety of boards on the walls. To these were hastily added information from the scene of Rasul's death on Frontenac Road.

Notes, including numerous circles and arrows in a variety of colours, had been scribbled on the boards as officers worked to make sense of the murders. Ouellette thought irreverently that the main board resembled a game plan for a football match.

Liz looked for a moment at the cluster of intent faces before her. Then she began. "Alright, so now Laila Daudova's husband, Rasul Daudov, has been shot dead—this morning, at about 6:45, according to a very frightened passer by. Forensics hasn't much to say as yet, but it looks similar to the attack on his wife. Shot from a distance, apparently from across the street, alongside a derelict building."

Ouellette added, "Again, no shell casing found."

Liz nodded. "But this time, at least, we have some footprints. The snow was soft enough, but they are pretty fuzzy and degraded. Greg, you'll follow up on that? In fact, get what you can from the crime scene investigators later in the day and brief me, yes?"

Greg Gibson nodded. Of course he would. This was the kind of stuff he lived for. Nothing ever seemed to happen in this dozy Canadian capital. This case was far more interesting than anything he had worked on recently. He took a quick swig of coffee to disguise his excitement.

Forsyth continued. "I know that some of you may be wondering if all of this is some sort of international conspiracy or some intelligence matter. I'm wondering the same thing but have no information on that score." She shot a glance at Lawrence Fletcher of CSIS, who was sitting at the back of room, gazing at a wall and giving every appearance of paying Liz no attention whatsoever. Fletcher never contributed anything to the meetings but attended every one, with all the charisma of a hall monitor.

"We must continue to investigate these deaths as we would any other homicide. Keep going after the Daudovs' finances—money transfers, contacts with criminal gangs, that sort of thing. Dissention within the Chechen community. Sexual secrets. In that connection, Cormier," here Liz regarded a veteran female constable, "take another look at the relationship between Daudov and Madina—something could be a bit off there.

"The press is all over this like a rash, and the Super's been fielding phone calls from the Prime Minister's Office and the Privy Council Office. So the sooner we get to the bottom of this the better, and the better we'll all sleep."

After the meeting, Forsyth and Ouellette sat together in silence. Then Liz said, "Gilles, I want you to get in touch with Canadian Immigration, border control, whoever has the information. Get me a list of everyone from Russia and the former Soviet Union who has arrived in Canada over the past six months."

Ouellette looked quizzically at his boss, then asked, "Legally or illegally?"

Liz grinned, probably for the first time that day. "Whatever you can get."

ELEVEN
England

Two other murders had been committed in Battersea since that of Sophie Bouchard, and the lack of information surrounding her murder was rendering the investigation stale. The battering death of a woman in what appeared to be a domestic dispute, in addition to the stabbing death of a young man outside a sleazy nightclub, meant that some resources would soon be diverted from the Bouchard case. Hay dreaded the regular phone calls from Sophie's mother, Marie, which must have been costing her a small fortune in long distance charges. Especially as he had virtually nothing new to tell her.

Hay returned to his office after bringing his superintendent up to date. His phone rang before he had a chance to sit down.

"Hay," he said, picking up the phone and dropping into the swivel chair.

"Hello, Chief Inspector," said a female voice at the other end of the phone. "My name is Luba Boswell." The woman took a deep breath and continued. "I would like to offer my help in solving the murder of the young Canadian woman, Sophie Bouchard."

Hay leaned over his desk and pressed the phone closer to his ear. Was there finally a lead, maybe even a break in this frustrating case? Might he finally have something to tell Marie Bouchard? What did this woman have to say? These thoughts and others were tumbling around his head as he said, "Thank you for calling. What is it you would like to tell us?"

"I think it would be best to meet in person," she replied.

Nothing unusual in that, thought Hay.

The woman continued nervously, "You see, I'm a psychic medium and I would prefer to deal face to face."

Hay slumped back in the chair, his mood instantly darkening. *Oh, for God's sake.*

"I see," he said.

"I wouldn't be calling unless I really thought I could help."

She had a soft, low voice and sounded genuine, but Hay had already developed a mental image of someone sitting in a dimly lit booth on Blackpool Pier, wearing huge hoop earrings and, most likely, staring into a crystal ball.

"Now, Miss . . ."

"Boswell. Luba Boswell. No doubt you are skeptical about people like me. But I am having some very strong, persistent impressions about this woman's death. And you don't have any other leads, do you?"

Hay reflected that it didn't take a psychic to work that one out but had to admit, at least to himself, that she was right. He took down her particulars and told her, somewhat reluctantly, that someone would be in touch. As he hung up the phone, he thought, *This sounds like a job for Wilkins.*

To Hay's surprise, Wilkins expressed interest in his new assignment.

"Not that I believe in this stuff, Sir. And of course there are a lot of cranks about. But Gemma is very keen on anything paranormal, and sometimes I do wonder if there isn't, well, something else. Sir." He finished this last thought quickly, noting the slightly raised eyebrows of his boss. "Probably a load of rubbish, though," he added.

"Well, here you go then," said Hay, handing his DS the note he had scribbled of Luba Boswell's coordinates.

Susan Beck from Penicuik in Scotland was quite possibly happier than she had ever been in her life. She was delighted to be on holiday, delighted to be in London, delighted to be away from home—*really* away from home—for the first time in her twenty-one years. Free from her nagging mother and alcoholic father, away from the constant criticism about everything: her ambitions, her friends, her weight. *Free, single and twenty-one*, she thought. *Doesn't get any better than that!*

Unfortunately, Susan Beck was also lost. She knew she couldn't be too far from her hostel but had obviously taken a wrong turn somewhere. This wasn't an area with which she was familiar. It looked a bit down at heel, almost abandoned. There weren't many birds to be heard, and while there was a constant roar of traffic, it sounded a long way off.

Susan had visited many of the usual tourist places the previous week: the Tower, the Victoria and Albert, Buckingham Palace . . . the list went on. It was ironic that she had navigated so many tourist destinations without a single misstep and then, going for a simple walk in the neighbourhood of her hostel, managed to get lost.

She smiled. She couldn't be so very far from her hostel; this was just another adventure on her journey. As she was pulling a tourist map from her knapsack, a skinny young man carrying a black sports bag approached her and asked, "Can I help you?"

Susan felt slightly nervous, but this was an American, it seemed (by his accent), and she was lost. And it was broad daylight, after all.

"I'm looking for the Willkommen Hostel, on Water Street." She smiled and added, "Just took a wrong turn or something."

"I know the Willkommen," said the young man with a smile. "You're not that far at all. I can walk you back."

"Okay," said Susan, tucking her map back inside the pocket of her knapsack. They introduced themselves, and she walked with him along several quiet streets. If she had harboured any concerns about her companion, they evaporated as soon as her surroundings began to look familiar.

She'd had enough of walking for one day and was getting very tired. Presently the man pointed out the Willkommen, which was just a couple of doors down. She thanked him and said goodbye, though a bit sadly. He had been good company.

DS Richard Wilkins, accompanied by PC Etheridge, pressed the buzzer in the entryway of the apartment building. It was a newish building in a quiet, residential area. This surprised Wilkins, although he had never before wondered what sort of money psychic mediums made. They were buzzed in and took the elevator to the fifth-floor flat occupied by Luba Boswell.

The flat was spacious and attractive. Numerous prints and paintings adorned dark, panelled walls. Most of the paintings featured winged creatures and dainty female forms. Wilkins wondered if Ms. Boswell had painted them herself—there was a certain dream-like quality to them. Several tall bookshelves were filled with hardcover books, and the hardwood floors boasted good quality Middle Eastern carpets. Wilkins and Etheridge followed Luba Boswell into her large, somewhat cluttered office.

There was nothing particularly elegant or ethereal about Luba herself. She was short, wide, and round, and her face was of similar proportions. She was plainly attired in a brown pantsuit and cream blouse with large lapels. Her dark hair was drawn up in a bun, and no make up embellished her plain, pleasant features. Wilkins supposed her to be in her late forties. Luba gestured to two chairs in front of her desk, and the officers sat across from the self-described psychic medium.

"Thank you very much for coming," she began, a bit hesitantly. She was accustomed to dealing with people who came to her because of her abilities. It was unusual to be called on by people whom, she suspected, didn't believe she was genuine. Luba Boswell had never had dealings of any kind with the police before.

"As you know from your chief inspector," she continued, "I am a psychic medium. I know the police in general don't believe in psychics, but sometimes people with psychic abilities have proven useful to the police."

She looked hopefully at the two young men across from her, and Wilkins smiled. He very much hoped that this woman would be the real deal—whatever that was—but he was doubtful. PC Etheridge, who was not remotely interested in anything he couldn't see with his own eyes, found this a colossal waste of time. Etheridge had to concentrate on his note-taking, however, as his spelling abilities were challenged by Luba's next declaration.

"I am clairvoyant, clairaudient, and clairsentient," she stated. "That means," she added with a quick smile towards Etheridge, "that I can see, hear, and feel impressions from people who have passed from this dimensional plane to the next."

"And you believe," said Wilkins, "that you have received information about Sophie Bouchard, the young woman murdered behind the Mallard Council Estate?"

Luba nodded, absently shuffling some papers in front of her. "From her. She is very upset."

Of course she is, thought Etheridge, having given up on his spelling. *She's dead.*

"She's upset about her mother," Luba continued. "Her mother, Sophie tells me, is frantic with worry and won't rest until this case is solved."

No surprise there, thought Wilkins. *Of course the mother is upset. Who wouldn't be?*

Luba stopped riffling through the papers and became still, staring intently at an item on her desk. She picked up a chain from which dangled a small crystal orb.

Oh gawd, not a crystal ball, thought Etheridge. *Although it's very small. She must be a rookie.*

Luba's eyes glazed over and she twirled the pendant in her chubby fingers. "She's showing me a young man, thin. Friend, she thought. She's telling me that she is just the first. That he must be stopped or he will do this again."

Wilkins stared hard at the woman. She looked sincere and quite possibly believed what she was saying. But could it be true?

"She is very strong, very insistent that the police must not forget her, or these things will continue."

"So who did it, then?" broke in Etheridge, with just a touch of impatience in his voice. He didn't notice the look of warning that Wilkins gave him.

"Thin, she says. Foreign? Maybe. She seems confused about that. He is here now, though. He was away but now he's back." Suddenly Luba's face cleared and she said, "I'm so sorry. I had no intention of going into a trance. She is very strong." Luba shook her head. "I was only going to tell you what she had told me before, but she insisted on telling you herself."

Wilkins didn't quite know how to reply, so he muttered

that no apology was necessary and thanked her for calling in with her information. As they were leaving, Luba Boswell gazed up into Wilkins's face and said, "Your lady. She is very beautiful, yes?"

Wilkins, confused, nodded.

"Has a name like Amber . . . Ruby?" Wilkins didn't reply but suddenly felt cold. "Very beautiful. Kind, smart lady. But not the right one for you. Don't move too fast. She is not the right one."

DCI Hay and DS Wilkins were attending the London première of a Canadian jazz dance company, at the invitation of Acting High Commissioner Rochon. A reception was held prior to the performance at the theatre, in an elegant hall illuminated by several large chandeliers. The walls were yellow, and tall, gold-framed mirrors graced one wall. The effect, to Hay, was of glittering light bouncing and shimmering throughout the room.

"Well," said Wilkins. "This is nice." Both detectives accepted glasses of wine proffered by a passing waiter. Wilkins, having procured some sort of meatball on a stick, was now attempting to dip it into a small dish of red sauce, while simultaneously holding onto a napkin and trying not to spill his wine. He succeeded, but only just, then quickly waved away a waiter holding a large tray of skewered shrimp.

Hay's mind wandered to the last elegant reception he had attended, the huge Christmas affair held at the Official Residence the previous month. He, Wilkins, and Liz hadn't lasted very long, partly because they felt out of place, but largely because of the phone call from Sergeant Gilles

Ouellette in Ottawa, which had led to the resolution of the Guévin murder. Liz had looked wonderful that night, he remembered, but these pleasant ruminations were interrupted by a "glad you could make it" from Paul Rochon, who was approaching, glass of wine in hand.

At the same time, Wilkins recognized one of the High Commission staff he had met during the previous investigation, and turned to speak with her.

Rochon said to Hay confidentially, "Luciano asked if you were coming." Luciano Alfredo Carillo was the extremely talented, if excitable, High Commission chef. Hay learned that Carillo had personally overseen the catering for this event, and that he "particularly recommends that you try the salmon and dill en croûte. You certainly made an impression on him as a man of fine taste."

"If he knew what sort of thing I eat most nights, he'd change his opinion of me pretty quickly," said Hay with a smile. "But please do thank him for me."

"Will do," said Rochon.

"By the way," added Hay. "I want to thank you as well."

"Me? What for?"

"I can only imagine that your authorities and the press are all over you for information about the Bouchard case. Thanks for not pushing us on that score. You know we're doing all we can, so thanks for just letting us try to get on with the job."

Rochon shrugged. "Some people expect miracles. And it's quite a sensational case, so people are naturally interested. But what would be the point of pressuring you or the Yard when I know you're doing what you can? I just hope

that one day we can get the answers that Mme Bouchard needs. That's all that matters."

Hay nodded and shook Rochon's hand warmly. The lights dimmed briefly, indicating that it was ten minutes until the performance, so Hay and Wilkins entered the theatre to take their seats.

Paul Rochon returned from the jazz dance performance to his luxurious flat in London. He could have moved into the official residence in the absence of a replacement High Commissioner but thought it would look pretentious to the rest of the staff. Besides, he liked his own place, with paintings and books and items of furniture that he recognized. They had accompanied him on many foreign postings and were sometimes the only things providing much comfort, especially in the tougher, hardship postings. He had learned that diplomats from some other countries designated Ottawa a hardship posting, based on the weather. He couldn't honestly disagree with that.

It was almost midnight, according to the carriage clock on the mantelpiece. He had visited with the dancers following the performance and confirmed that they had all been pleased with the evening. *It was a good performance*, Paul acknowledged to himself, *but it would have been awfully nice to have spent an evening at home, maybe doing something mindless like watching television.*

He took off his stiff formal attire and changed into his nightclothes. He poured himself a short scotch and sank into the couch in an attempt to unwind from the day's events. Paul knew he had an early start in the morning, but, he thought, when *hadn't* he had an early start? He was stressed, exhausted, and lonely. He wasn't particularly surprised when the phone rang.

Ottawa, he thought grimly. Which it was, but not with any inquiries about the Bouchard case. A successor to Wesley Carruthers was finally being proposed. Of course, the British government would have to accept the nomination of the new High Commissioner, but that would just be a formality.

Paul's heart sank when he heard the name of the new Head of Post: Lucien Roy—a flack and party bagman of the highest order. He was a political insider and great friend of the sitting prime minister. And reportedly a nasty piece of work to boot.

The director of the Heads of Post section of Personnel tried to break the news gently to Paul, telling him how excellent it would be for the post to practically have the ear of the prime minister; that Roy's recommendations to Ottawa were virtually guaranteed to be acted upon; that Roy was clearly held in high regard by the party.

When Paul hung up the phone, however, he knew what he really had to look forward to. And that was working for someone with no diplomatic experience or even government experience, possessed of unbending and politicized opinions, and a reportedly vicious temper. Paul topped up his scotch.

TWELVE
Canada

Madina Grigoryeva lived in a two-storey walk-up near King Edward with an older sister and a male cousin who had entered Canada close to three years prior to Madina's arrival in the nation's capital. The blue-eyed Chechen woman regularly demonstrated in front of the Russian Embassy.

Cousin Aslan had, in fact, immigrated to Canada legally. He had filled out the paperwork, attended the interviews, and provided proof of a job offer in Canada. He was proud that Canada saw him as a desirable immigrant. He had even learned French in his spare time back in Chechnya. As a result, he felt somewhat superior to many of his Chechen compatriots, and even members of his own family, who had entered by different routes. Aslan was agitated by the presence of the Canadian police in his home and decided it would be best to say nothing.

Madina invited Liz and Ouellette to sit at a small wooden dining table. They learned that Madina's sister was at work. Cousin Aslan, a corpulent man who appeared to be in his forties, had withdrawn to a corner of the room when the detectives arrived. He sat in a deep armchair, crossed his arms across his broad chest, and silently observed the proceedings.

Madina was perhaps in her early twenties, with those remarkable, ice-blue eyes and long, glossy hair. She spoke in halting but very correct English.

"I am sorry you had trouble finding me. The apartment is in Aslan's name," she said, gesturing towards the brooding, silent man seated in the corner.

"You were at the Russian Embassy the day Laila Daudova was shot, yes?" Liz began.

"Yes," replied Madina. "My husband disappeared from Grozny three years ago. Finally Cousin Aslan and my sister convinced me to come to Canada. They said it was hopeless to try to find Hamid."

"So, how long have you been here?" asked Ouellette. He noticed a furtive glance exchanged between Madina and her cousin, and wondered again just how some of these people actually made it into Canada.

"One year," she replied.

"Have you found work?" asked Liz conversationally.

"Sometimes, as a Russian translator. Some documents

from companies doing business in Russia. Aslan has contacts," she said with another nod towards the immobile Aslan.

"Did you know Laila Daudova well?" asked Liz.

"No," said Madina flatly.

"Yet it was you who went to inform Mr. Daudov of the death of his wife."

Madina coloured a little and nodded. "Yes," she said, "I knew Mr. Daudov—Rasul—better than I knew Laila."

"Why was that?" asked Liz.

"We both attend a small community group where Chechens can meet and talk together. We meet about once a month, at our different homes. Discuss events in the old country, talk about how to get along here, find work."

"And Laila did not attend these meetings?"

"No," replied Madina. "Rasul said she was not interested to come. I attended with my sister and cousin."

"That's how you got to know Mr. Daudov?"

Madina nodded. Liz noticed that Cousin Aslan had begun shifting his considerable weight about in his chair.

"Is it true," asked Liz, "that Rasul Daudov did not approve of his wife attending the demonstrations?"

Madina nodded again. "He was worried that she might become a target of the Russians." She blushed more deeply. "He was right, perhaps." She thought for a moment, then added, "So that was why I went to tell Rasul. It was his worst fear, and I thought it would be best if I told him before the police came."

No, Madina had heard nothing, seen nothing unusual on the day of Laila's death—nothing until the crack of the bullet. The demonstration had been small that day; most people had stayed home due to the ice storm. Madina told Liz and Ouellette that, to some extent, she knew Omar Glausov—the man whose twin was missing—because he sometimes came to the monthly meetings as well. She didn't know the elderly Mrs. Umarova well at all. Madina had absolutely no idea why the people from Independence United attended the demonstrations, and had never spoken to them.

As Liz and Ouellette drove back to the office, Ouellette wondered aloud if something might have been going on between Madina Grigoryeva and Rasul Daudov.

"I was thinking the same thing," said Liz, "especially as Cousin Aslan seemed uncomfortable when Rasul's name came up. But even if there was some sort of romantic involvement, Madina was demonstrating in front of the embassy at the time. And she certainly doesn't come across as a killer."

"Agreed," said Ouellette, "and it's hard to imagine her organizing a gun-for-hire scheme to get Laila out of the way. But stranger things have happened."

Liz couldn't argue with that.

They got out of the squad car and climbed the slippery front steps of the RCMP office on Cooper. It was already eleven in the morning but still sixteen below. A stiff westerly wind made it feel even colder. They entered the front doors accompanied by a blast of freezing air, and stomped the snow off their boots. The constable at the front desk caught Liz's eye.

"That girl," he said with a jerk of his head, "says she wants to speak with you about the Daudova case. She calls herself

Mila . . ." He double-checked his notes. ". . . Kras-ni-ye-va."

Liz and Ouellette spun around to see none other than the flame-haired siren, the spiritual leader of Independence United. She rose and approached the detectives, her long black coat sweeping along behind her.

"I have to speak with you. You see, I *did* actually see something on the day that Laila Daudova was murdered."

A few moments later, the three were seated in an interview room. Ouellette pulled out his well-thumbed notebook and began writing.

"Well, it's like this," said Mila. She seemed uncharacteristically nervous. "I told the others that I couldn't attend the demonstration that day because I had other business to attend to. That wasn't entirely true. Although I guess it was, in a way . . ." She gazed at a wall, apparently trying to determine exactly what it was she meant to say.

"What were you doing instead?" Liz prompted.

"Well, I did in fact go to the Russian Embassy."

Ouellette glanced up, puzzled.

"I got off the bus a couple of stops early and walked towards the embassy on Charlotte. Then I sort of hid behind one of the houses across the street. There never seems to be anyone in those houses. I think the people must be away a lot."

"Why were you hiding?" asked Liz, genuinely interested.

"I wanted to make sure that Tony, Pierre, and Andrea actually turned up at the demonstration." She coloured a bit and said, "Sometimes, you see, I wonder if all of them are as committed as they say they are. Sometimes they've not told me the truth about what they're doing in support of the cause. I've become a bit, well, wary about a couple of my colleagues. Some of them seem to have other agendas."

No shit, thought Ouellette.

"I've sometimes even wondered if some of them might be government plants," she said, looking suspiciously at Liz and Ouellette.

Ouellette kept his head down, taking notes and smiling to himself. *Can she really imagine that her little gang of misfits is important enough to warrant planting an informant?*

Liz wondered if the woman was a bit paranoid. *Really, spying on her supposedly like-minded supporters to ensure they were actually freezing their butts off in support of Chechen independence?* Instead Liz said, "And were they all there? Tony, Pierre, and Andrea?"

The girl shook her head slowly.

"Well, no," she admitted, "but that's not why I'm here."

"But they weren't all there," said Liz. "Who was missing?"

Mila regarded Liz dubiously but answered the question.

"It was Tony. Tony wasn't there."

"Tony Blackwell," said Ouellette, remembering the young man they had met in the grubby basement apartment along with his confederates from Independence United.

Mila nodded. Liz asked her if she knew where Blackwell was when he was meant to be at the demonstration.

"No," answered Mila.

"And did you confront him later about his absence?"

"No."

"Did Pierre or Andrea tell you that he hadn't shown up?"

"No," said Mila, annoyed at this evident lack of loyalty.

Liz made a mental note to re-interview the young anarchist about his whereabouts on the morning of Laila Daudova's murder.

"So," continued Liz, "what did you want to tell us? You said that you saw something while you were watching from the other side of the street."

The girl nodded. "I hadn't been there long. I saw that Pierre and Andrea were there and that Tony wasn't. I was really mad. I trusted Tony. I was about to go back home—it was awfully cold. Really damp," she said with an involuntary shudder. "Then I heard what I thought was a small explosion and I saw the poor woman drop. It was, of course, the gunshot, although I've never actually heard one before."

She glanced up at Liz, who was thinking that the girl looked very young and quite frightened. Mila continued. "It sounded as if the shot had come from nearby. I sort of froze, but I looked towards where I thought the shot had come from and I saw a man walking quickly away from the back of the next house."

"Walking?" asked Liz. "After just shooting someone?"

"It sounds strange," agreed Mila Krasniyeva, "but it was very, very slippery. The ice had hardened on top of the snow and it was like a skating rink over there. I was having trouble staying upright and was just standing still."

Liz nodded. That was the reason there had been no footprints. "And he didn't see you?"

"No. And I didn't see him until I heard the shot. We were both, I guess, in hiding."

Good thing you didn't pick the same spot, thought Liz. "That's quite the coincidence."

"Well, yes, it was," said the girl with a small shrug. "But no, he didn't see me at all, and after the shot he turned away and headed in the other direction. He didn't actually seem to be looking around at all, come to think of it. He certainly didn't look nervous."

"Why didn't you tell us about your visit to the embassy before?" asked Ouellette.

Mila flushed. "I didn't want the others to know what I was up to. That I didn't trust them." She thought for a moment, then added, "And of course we have a great deal of suspicion about the authorities in general." Now she was on more comfortable ground. Lifting her chin and squaring her shoulders, she pronounced, "The state authorities are devoted solely to keeping and expanding their own power and safe guarding the regime. We believe that the police are—wittingly or not—a part of the apparatus that is designed to keep the peoples under the thumb of the state . . ."

Mila had hit her stride. Before either detective had a chance to intervene, they were treated to another extended diatribe direct from the manifesto of Independence United, if such a document existed. Liz could have interrupted but reminded herself that the girl had come in of her own accord; if the young woman wanted to launch into a polemic, it might be best to listen politely for a minute or two.

Ouellette pretended to take notes but was in fact scribbling a number of insulting phrases in colloquial French that would prove difficult for anyone else to decipher.

Liz diplomatically stifled a yawn and finally interjected, "And the shooter was definitely a man?"

"Definitely."

"Did you get a good look at him?"

"Not really, no."

Liz cocked her head.

"He was about average height and build," said Mila. "Wearing one of those ugly puffy ski jackets that look like a lot of stuffed patches sewn together. Dark. You know the kind—they were popular in the seventies, I think. Some kind of fur hat. He was carrying a duffel bag."

"Would the bag have been big enough to hold a rifle?"

"No idea. I only saw it from the back."

"Then what did you do?"

"I think I must have been in shock or something. I started walking quickly back the way I came. By the time I thought to catch the bus I was already halfway home."

They sent her off to give a statement, and Liz and Ouellette looked vacantly at each other.

"Interesting," commented Ouellette once Mila had flounced out of the room.

"Yes," agreed Liz. "Except all we have is a pretty useless description. And an indication that Krasniyeva is either paranoid or not as silly as she sounds. In any event, we'll need to talk to Blackwell again. Find out why he lied to Mila and where he was at the time of the shooting."

Ouellette nodded. "They're a weird bunch of kids. But what motive could Blackwell have to kill Laila? He was supposed to be supporting her cause."

Liz shoved her hair back from her face, vaguely realizing that she was overdue for a trim.

"Perhaps it *is* political," ventured Ouellette. "In which case . . ."

"We're out of our depth," agreed Liz. "But for the moment, let's just focus on the crimes. We'll talk to Blackwell as soon as possible. I also want to find out if there was anything going on between Rasul Daudov and Madina Grigoryeva."

"Yes, Sir," said Ouellette with a grin. He knew his boss hated being called "Ma'am" and this case was clearly getting her down. Him too, for that matter.

Liz smiled and reached for her jacket. "Let's go for it, then."

At the end of a long day, Liz collected Rochester from the Greens' house. As usual, she declined their kind offer of a glass of wine or a cup of tea. It was late and she was dead tired. Rochester licked Liz's face as she bent down to greet him, then looked at her intently as though he would have loved to go for a run. It was ten o'clock, and the last thing Liz felt like at the moment (or any other time, for that matter) was to go for a run. So the two of them walked to the house in silence. Rochester bounded through the back door, trotted up to the fireplace, walked in three circles, lay down, and went to sleep. Pouring herself a glass of Cabernet, Liz looked enviously at her dog. She wished that she could just turn around three times and fall fast asleep as well, but her head was spinning.

Half an hour later she was beginning to unwind and was watching a television programme. A pretty, happy-looking woman was demonstrating how to use stencils to brighten up cupboards and walls. Liz looked around at her walls and decided that her landlord would be unimpressed if he walked in to find the place covered with butterflies and flowers. Still, she found herself somehow drawn to the woman on the television, who was now constructing an elaborate table setting. The woman was intent on beautifying the things around her, and had a serene and joyful presence. Liz was surprised that she was envious, even though she knew that she would be bored brainless by stencilling bluebirds or arranging flowers. But at a time like this, such things seemed immensely more pleasurable than trying to find an assassin who, for all intents and purposes, had disappeared as soon as he had killed.

Rochester yipped in his sleep, dreaming. Liz sometimes wondered what dogs dreamed about and how they understood the difference between dreams and reality. Some humans seemed unable to make that distinction, but she had observed that both dogs and horses dreamed, and then seemed to carry on as normal once they awoke.

Now the television woman was painting, freehand, a rose on a glass vase. Liz wandered into the kitchen and refilled her glass. When she slumped back down onto the couch, the crafty lady had been replaced by an equally pretty, happy-looking woman describing how to make a three-course meal for four in under half an hour.

Liz awoke suddenly from a nightmare that rendered her body numb and immobile. Her heart was pounding, she was drenched in sweat, and she felt nauseated. She sometimes thought that the ancients were right: not everything was in the brain. For her, emotion was lodged firmly in the viscera.

She was sleeping terribly tonight. Whenever she did get to sleep, she was awoken by a nightmare. This was the second in as many hours. She looked at the clock and decided she might be able to eke out a bit more sleep. Then, her thoughts clearing slightly, she wondered whether it had been a nightmare or an idea.

Frowning, she got out of bed. She had a drink of water and, returning to bed, tried again to sleep.

THIRTEEN

Canada

At Liz's direction, Ouellette called the Ottawa offices of Citizenship and Immigration first thing. She had asked him to determine when and where any Russians—specifically Chechens—had entered Canada within the past six months. Ouellette had been referred to the director general of the Case Management Branch. Since the young sergeant had been invited to come over right away, the grave, middle-aged woman had been allowed little time to prepare. She was clearly a pro, however, swiftly reviewing a series of files and pattering on the keyboard of her computer.

Ouellette had to amuse himself with a cup of coffee,

which had been delivered by a haughty-looking secretary who clearly found the task beneath her. She flipped untidy hair impatiently as she left the office, obviously having better things to do.

After about fifteen minutes, Ms. Stephanie Sayward swivelled her desk chair in Ouellette's direction and, in a surprisingly high-pitched voice, asked, "It's basically Chechens you're interested in, yes?"

"Yes," agreed Ouellette, "although if you have a list of other Russians visiting or immigrating during that period, that would be useful as well."

Ms. Sayward nodded slowly, regarding Ouellette intently. "I am not at all comfortable in divulging this information," she said, to Ouellette's surprise.

"Why not?" he asked, placing his coffee cup on a nearby credenza.

"Privacy legislation," she said, still inspecting Ouellette. "These people are subject to the same privacy protections as you and me once they enter the country."

Ouellette thought quickly. He had not expected to be stonewalled by a government official and was genuinely surprised by the reach of Canada's privacy laws. He met her gaze steadily and said slowly, "This is a murder investigation, Ms. Sayward—and a very complex one at that. We need your help."

Ms. Sayward was silent for a moment, reflecting on what the young sergeant had just said. She was prepared to cooperate and to defend her decision if required. Anyway, she was retiring soon. She didn't have much to lose.

She exhaled deeply and said, "A list of all Russian

visitors will take some time to compile. And it won't give you a complete picture—we only have records on those who would have been sent for secondary examination by Customs. But yes, I can give you what I have, including the immigrants."

Sayward paused and adjusted her glasses. "Of course, there are always those who manage to get in with fake visas, or fake or stolen passports. It doesn't happen a lot, but it does happen. Most of the forgeries are pretty amateurish but some are extremely good. We have no record of people entering like that, unless they get caught. I do have three male Chechens, who entered independently of one another."

"How did you get *that* information so quickly?" asked Ouellette, intrigued.

"Separate data base," she said. "All three claimed refugee status on arrival. Religious grounds. Claimed they were being persecuted due to their Muslim faith. Each was given a date for a hearing and allowed to leave."

"Can you tell me where and when they arrived?"

Ms. Sayward rotated her chair and peered at her monitor. "One arrived in Montreal, at Mirabel, in November 1997. The two others came into Toronto, one in August 1997 and another in . . . yes . . . December. I can give you the names in a minute. I'll write them down because I can't pronounce them."

Ouellette was prepared to grin, but Ms. Sayward was only citing fact and had no intention of making a joke. So he just nodded and asked, "Does the department follow up on the whereabouts of refugee claimants prior to their hearings?"

"Not especially, unless they're of particular concern. We don't have the resources to do that. And, for that matter, neither do you," she said matter-of-factly. She resumed work at her keyboard.

She was right about that, Ouellette thought. He was about to ask another question but Sayward continued. "They self-report, though. The file on one of the fellows who entered at Toronto is quite lengthy," she said with a nod at the screen. "He seems to have wanted to notify the authorities every time he sneezed—presumably so he does nothing to jeopardize his refugee claim. The other who came in at Toronto seems to be living with . . ." she pattered on her keyboard for another moment, "a relative in Etobicoke." This seemed to strike Sayward as odd, as she raised her eyebrows and gave her head a small shake.

"And the one who came in at Montreal?"

Another bit of pattering and then, "He seems to have claimed he had friends in—well, how about that?—Gatineau, just across the river. Apparently he would be going there directly from Mirabel. That's the last we have on him."

Ouellette would have loved a refill and a further discussion of this fascinating world but wasn't about to risk the ire of the secretary, so he satisfied himself with obtaining the full names of the refugee claimants, their particulars, and the dates of their hearings. Sayward undertook to provide him the rest of the information on Russian visitors and immigrants as soon as possible, and he headed back to the office. He wasn't entirely sure what his boss wanted this information for, but it had been an interesting interview.

Due to his early meeting, Ouellette arrived just as the daily task force meeting was breaking up. He explained to Liz that his meeting at Immigration had started earlier than he had expected.

"They said to come over right away. I tried to call to tell you I'd miss the task force meeting but I think your cell phone is dead."

"Wretched things," she muttered. They had all recently been issued cell phones, for police purposes only, but Liz rarely remembered to charge hers. "Might as well be on a leash. Anyway, what did you find out?"

"We'll be getting more information later, but meanwhile we have details of three Chechen males who arrived in the past few months and claimed refugee status."

Ouellette filled her in on the details of his visit to Immigration.

"Interesting," she said, looking at the names Ouellette had been given by Ms. Sayward. "One of these fellows, the one living in Gatineau, is named Rasul. Coincidence, perhaps. Is it a common Chechen name?"

"No use asking me," replied the sergeant with a grin. "I don't even know where to start with the pronunciation of these guys' names."

"Me neither," agreed Liz. "Look, talk to Holmes," she said, referring to one of the Ontario Provincial Police members of the task force. "Ask the OPP to follow up on the two Chechen fellows living in Ontario, and we'll follow up with this Rasul in Gatineau."

"What are we trying to find out? And why?"

"Just what they're up to in general—if they've heard about

Laila's death, and if they have any suspicions. They're so new to the country that they're probably trying to reach out to their compatriots and are probably being told more than we are."

Ouellette nodded.

"And I'm also starting to wonder . . ." began Liz. She was interrupted by the sudden appearance of a constable in the doorway.

"Excuse me, Ma'am," he said. "But the Super wants you to come up and give him a briefing on the task force meeting. He says he was trying to call you on your cell phone but couldn't get through."

Liz rolled her eyes at Ouellette and left the room.

Tony Blackwell, nominally the spokesman of the Canadian chapter of Independence United, was surprised to see Liz and her sergeant at his door once again. This time Blackwell was alone and, without his cohort, seemed very young and very nervous. He invited them to sit on the same frilly cushions as before, and he perched on the edge of a worn, corduroy couch.

"So, what can I do for you?" asked Blackwell with an unconvincing smile.

"Mr. Blackwell," Liz began. "We understand that you were not, in fact, in attendance during the demonstration in front of the Russian Embassy on the day that Laila Daudova was shot."

Blackwell's eyes opened wide in shock, then he quickly tried to recover his calm demeanour.

"Who told you that?" he asked, with a mixture of fear and defiance.

"That doesn't matter," said Liz. "But you admit you weren't there?"

"Yes," said Blackwell, almost inaudibly.

"Where were you?"

"Here," said Blackwell with a small shrug, indicating his meagre surroundings.

"With anyone?"

"No."

"So why didn't you go to the demonstration?" asked Ouellette.

Blackwell stared at the knobbly carpet for a moment. Then he looked up and regarded Ouellette anxiously.

"It was cold, horrible. Windy. Things weren't at all back to normal after the ice storm. It just seemed like, you know, a hassle to get there."

"Perhaps," Liz prodded gently, "you are not as committed to the organization as some others? Like Mila maybe?"

Despite his abundance of facial hair, it was clear that Blackwell was blushing.

"Of course I am committed," he said, with an attempt at defiance. "I completely support the aims of the organization. Independence is an indisputable . . ."

Ouellette, unwilling to endure yet another lecture from the Independence United handbook, broke in.

"Can anyone confirm that you were here at the time of Laila Daudova's death?"

Blackwell inhaled quickly. "Perhaps," he faltered, "my landlord. He lives upstairs. He doesn't work much. Maybe he was home—I'm not sure. Or maybe his wife. But she works . . ." he trailed off, confused.

"So why," continued Liz, "did your colleagues, Pierre and Andrea, remain silent when you said that the three of you had been at the demonstration?"

Blackwell gave a small smile. "Because all of us have skipped demonstrations at one time or another. Mila would have everybody at every demo in town if she had her way. She's a wonderful woman but quite, er, demanding." He flushed more deeply.

"And you want her to trust you," added Liz.

"I do," said Blackwell. "I would do anything for Mila. I don't want to let her down—she is so committed to the organization. It was just that morning, when I thought about catching the buses, going to the embassy. Were the diplomats even working that day? Maybe even they had stayed at home." He paused as something dawned on him, then gasped, "It wasn't Mila who told you that I wasn't there, was it? Did she know?" He was wide-eyed, panicked.

Liz nodded. "I'm afraid so. She knew that you hadn't turned up at the embassy that morning."

Blackwell closed his eyes and threw his head back in despair.

"Mr. Blackwell," Liz said, "did you kill Laila Daudova on the morning of January 12 outside the Russian Embassy?"

"Good God, no!" exclaimed Blackwell. "No, no, why would I do that? I'd never even spoken with her . . . oh, God, I see, you don't know where I was . . . but no, of course not!"

Blackwell looked like a boy whose young life was crumbling before him.

"So you deny any involvement in the murder of Laila Daudova?"

"No, absolutely not. Oh, no, I mean yes, I deny it," fumbled Blackwell.

"And you have no idea who might have committed the murder?"

"No, none, absolutely not."

"Thank you Mr. Blackwell," said Liz standing. "You have been very helpful. We can let ourselves out."

At 6:45 PM, Liz and Ouellette were sitting in an unmarked squad car outside a fleabag motel in Gatineau, at present the home of the Chechen refugee claimant who had entered at Montreal the previous November. The one calling himself Rasul, Liz reflected. Rasul Nikolayevich Nasarov. This was the second time they had run across the name Rasul during the investigation. Except that Rasul Daudov was dead, shot outside his apartment building not long after the murder of his wife, Laila.

The inspector and the sergeant were silent in the cold car, coffees in hand, doughnuts wrapped in brown paper bags. Liz had a double chocolate, and Ouellette had ordered a cinnamon twist. They felt like a couple of bad stereotypes. It was somewhere around twenty below, the sun had disappeared long ago, and this Rasul wasn't at the motel. The cold was exacerbated by the dampness, and the air was heavy.

They would wait, Liz thought grimly, as long as it took to interview this guy. They had initially spoken with the motel clerk, an elderly Québécois, then knocked on the door of number twelve, the Chechen's room. Getting no reply, she and Ouellette had gone to fetch coffee from a nearby doughnut shop. On their return to the motel they tried again, with the same result. They went back to the car. They had been waiting well over an hour.

"Where the hell is he?" muttered Liz, huddled into her coat. Ouellette only shook his head.

FOURTEEN
Canada

Clarice Eddington, fondly known to her colleagues as the "Silver Fox" due to her hair colour, was on the lookout for would-be shoplifters. As the senior store detective for a major department chain, she always had her eyes open for people with that tell-tale, shifty look. It was her job, and she took it seriously. *How on earth*, she sometimes wondered, *could cameras actually replace the experience of the store detective?* Yet she knew the change was coming, if gradually, and was grateful that her employer was among the last to abandon the detectives altogether.

Shoplifters were easy to spot and easy to catch, but

charging them could become quite complicated. Some were giggling gaggles of teenaged girls, hovering around the cosmetics department attempting to lift a lipstick. Then there were the pros, armed with empty shopping bags or even wearing the infamous "booster-bloomers," into which enormous quantities of merchandise could be deposited discreetly and rapidly. Some were the "regulars," well known to the detectives at all the major stores; others were members of staff who apparently felt entitled to take money from the till or pocket the odd cassette. Occasionally, obviously affluent women came in to pick up things they didn't need and could easily pay for. These were allegedly suffering from kleptomania, but Clarice didn't have much time for them. Others looked desperately poor, and often she was tempted to look the other way.

At present, Clarice was watching a scruffy, dark-complexioned man while she pretended to browse through the canned goods in the grocery department. His eyes darted left and right as he pocketed a few tins of fish. She followed him to the bakery aisle, maintaining a discreet distance as she watched him slip a packet of biscuits into his other pocket.

She had him. But she had to wait until he exited the store with the goods on him; otherwise charges wouldn't stick. And, too often, her boss was willing to let people go with a warning rather than call in the police.

Clarice looked around quickly for backup. A young, burly grocery clerk was watching her as he packed a customer's groceries. He had occasionally helped in the past. He loved this sort of thing. Clarice caught his eye and he nodded, immediately deserting the cashier and leaving her to do the packing on her own.

Now moving quite quickly, the suspect turned and started towards the exit. Clarice hurried along behind him.

A blast of icy air struck them both in the face as the doors opened. "Excuse me, sir," she said as they both went through the double doors at the same time. "I wonder if you'd mind coming up to the office."

Apparently he did mind, because he began running into the icy parking lot. The young grocery clerk was right behind them and, in the end, grabbed the shoplifter by the arm of his ski jacket. The suspect, looking up into the determined face of his captor, had no choice but to accept Clarice's invitation.

By the time that Clarice, her supervisor, and the shoplifter (or the *alleged* shoplifter, Clarice reminded herself with a sigh) were seated in the office, it became apparent that the suspect spoke neither English nor French. Clarice and Mr. Trevino had only been able to establish that the suspect spoke Russian—or, as he said "Ruski,"—and claimed himself unable to understand anything asked of him.

Clarice inclined her head towards her boss and said quietly that Irena from Cosmetics was of Russian heritage and might be able to serve as interpreter. Trevino, agreeing that Irena did indeed have some sort of accent, said that she should be called for.

The suspect shifted about unhappily in his chair, his dark eyes darting from Clarice to Trevino to the floor and back again. He was, thought Clarice, extremely nervous.

She wondered what his background was. Was this someone who shoplifted regularly or was it a one-off? Certainly she hadn't seen him before. She felt sure that she would have remembered him if she had. He had several days' growth of beard and a greyish pallor to his dark skin. His face looked almost like a carving, with deep lines running from his nose to his set mouth and continuing straight down to his chin. Nonetheless he did not appear very old. *Thirty at best,* thought Clarice.

The man's hands were thrust deep into his pockets, and his loot was assembled on the table before him. Clarice was surprised to find that what she had believed to be tinned fish was, in fact, caviar. Although the suspect appeared to have fallen on hard times, he clearly had refined tastes.

Irena Stuart knocked apprehensively on Mr. Trevino's door. Never before had she been called to the office of the Chief Loss Prevention Officer. What had she done? An extra splash of that lovely new perfume on her wrist, but that was only to let the customer have a good sniff—had she perhaps given away too many lipstick samples? Surely that wouldn't get her into trouble. Would it? She trembled, and beads of sweat broke out underneath the translucent powder on her forehead. The Silver Fox opened the door, and Irena relaxed a little, as she had always gotten on well with Clarice. But immediately she began to worry again. Surely Clarice didn't suspect her of something?

Soon, however, Irena's worries were put to rest, and she began first to breathe, then to feel quite important in her new role as interpreter. Irena was able to tell Clarice and her boss a little about the suspect. His name was Rasul Nasarov.

No, he wasn't carrying identification. He was from Moscow. He spoke only Russian. He had stolen nothing. If any stolen merchandise was on him, it had been planted. He would be happy to take the department store to court.

At this last statement, Mr. Trevino blanched and turned to Clarice. They exited the office together, leaving Mr. Nasarov and Irena alone together.

"For crying out loud," said Clarice, who swore but rarely, "I saw him take the stuff; it was on him when we got him in the office. It's open and shut."

"Yes, yes, I know," said Trevino, "but it's not a lot of money, is it? Is it worth going to court for?" he asked, wiping his brow with a yellowing handkerchief.

"Did you *see* the price on that caviar? Anyway, we have to inform the police. We can't just let this go when we have this much evidence."

Trevino very much wanted to go home. His shift was almost over, he was hungry, and court cases were a nightmare. But Clarice was right. They had to inform the police.

Clarice went back in to the office, her boss trailing glumly behind her. Irena told the suspect in Russian that he had to stay put and that charges would probably be laid. He threw back his head, shaking back his straggly locks. "Okay," he said proudly. Or, more precisely, he said "*harosho*," although the look in his eyes indicated that things were anything but harasho.

He didn't know why his friend and handler— another Chechen refugee claimant currently residing in Etobicoke—had told him to use the name of Rasul Nikolayevich Nasarov when he applied for refugee status in Canada; still, he followed the advice. His friend, with whom he had trained, seemed to know how these things operated. Now calling himself Rasul, he had been pleased to take his friend's advice and to prove to his handlers that he had the mettle to be a good plant. But he had his own, more personal reasons for wanting to come to Canada, and his actions would prove that he was a trustworthy and devout jihadist.

Irena left the office of the Chief Loss Prevention Officer in much better spirits than when she had entered. She was told that she might be called back later in the evening to interpret for the police. Squaring her shoulders and looking very professional, Irena smiled at the Silver Fox and nodded. Just prior to closing the door behind her, Irena commented to Clarice that "he has a bit of a Chechen accent, you know." Clarice didn't know but took a mental note. Although she wasn't altogether sure what "Chechen" meant.

Shortly thereafter, the shoplifter who spoke Russian with a Chechen accent found himself imprisoned in the main police station on Elgin Street. He was informed, via interpreter (not Irena from Cosmetics this time, but a professional from the Public Service), that the Russian Embassy would be informed of his predicament.

At this the suspect became infuriated. Even Police Constable Clarke understood the word *nyet*. The suspect repeated it several times most emphatically, followed by a torrent of incomprehensible words and a great many hand gestures. The interpreter turned to Clarke and explained that the suspect was not interested in any assistance from the embassy, that he was a Chechen and wanted nothing to do with the Russians.

Puzzled, Clarke asked of the interpreter, "Do we have a Chechen Embassy here?" which earned him a short lecture from the interpreter concerning the Chechen independence movement. Somewhat chastened but now better informed, Clarke contacted the RCMP liaison officer for the Russian Embassy, who immediately contacted Headquarters. The liaison officer also apprised the Russian Embassy duty officer of the events. The duty officer in turn phoned Cultural Attaché Stanislav Ivanov at his home on Island Park Drive. While Ivanov was not normally involved with consular work, it was well known at the embassy that he had taken a particular interest in the Daudova case and had stayed in contact with RCMP Inspector Liz Forsyth. It was natural that he should be informed about a Chechen running afoul of Canadian law.

Rasul Nikolayevich Nasarov still hadn't returned to the motel. Liz and Ouellette had decided they had no choice but to leave the car running—it was much too cold to switch off the engine for more than a moment or two. Suddenly the radio crackled in the squad car. Headquarters was relaying a message from the RCMP officer in charge of liaison between the police and several embassies.

Liz was interested to learn that a "suspicious person who might be of interest to you" was being held at the Elgin Street station on a shoplifting charge. Puzzled, Liz said that yes, she wanted to see him. Perhaps this would be more productive than sitting outside the apartment of the elusive Rasul Nasarov.

Ouellette was keen to get to the station as quickly as possible and prepared to drive off with lights blazing and sirens blaring. Liz shook her head and told her enthusiastic sergeant that it was far too slippery to go speeding through the streets of the national capital region.

Such a guy thing, she thought with an inward smile.

The RCMP liaison officer told Liz and Ouellette that a suspect was being held on shoplifting charges, and that the man identified himself as Rasul Nasarov. They were ushered into a small interview room. Liz and Ouellette regarded with interest the figure seated bolt upright in an evidently uncomfortable plastic chair. Although not a large man, the alleged shoplifter was muscular and appeared physically powerful. He was extremely tense and rubbed his hands together continually; the very air around him seemed charged with electricity. Despite his apparent physical strength, he looked sickly. His skin gave an overall impression of greyness. His hair was straggly and he was unkempt. The man raised his bloodshot eyes and regarded Liz and Ouellette with a combination of fear and defiance.

So this, thought Liz, *is why Rasul Nasarov didn't return to his apartment this evening.*

FIFTEEN
Canada

The man alleging to be Rasul Nikolayevich Nasarov did not want a lawyer. Nor did he want any assistance from the Russian Embassy. This was all made clear by the Public Service interpreter, who had accompanied Nasarov—or whatever his name was—during the evening's adventures. The interpreter was having a marvellous time. This was far more interesting than interpreting for pre-scripted state visits or tedious business deliberations.

All the same, the interpreter was definitely earning his fee. Nasarov's thoughts were disorganized and difficult to follow. His Chechen accent was extremely thick, making interpretation even more challenging.

Liz and Ouellette seated themselves opposite the shoplifter. Liz introduced herself and her sergeant, and the introductions were duly relayed by the interpreter. The man nodded to indicate he understood, briefly displaying bad teeth. Not a smile, thought Liz—it was something more akin to a snarl.

As it turned out, the suspect spoke English much better than these Canadian officials knew, but he was in such a state of nervous excitement that he couldn't have found the correct English words at the moment anyway. He rubbed his hands continually, as though washing them or as though reassuring himself that he was, indeed, here. At any rate, he had nothing to say to these people.

The man knew he had made a big mistake in stealing from the store. How was he to know that that grey-haired bitch was some sort of security person? She had worn no uniform. He felt a flash of anger towards his friend in Etobicoke—surely he could have warned him about this sort of thing?

The detectives sat at the green table across from the shoplifter, the interpreter seated on one long side. The RCMP liaison officer and Ottawa police constable had retreated to watch events from behind the two-way mirror, in case their services should be required.

"Ask him his name," said Liz, inclining her head towards the interpreter. She stared hard at the man, certain she had seen him before.

"*Ya uje govoril vam.* Rasul Nasarov."

"I already told you," was the interpretation, "Rasul Nasarov."

"You're staying at a motel in Gatineau, right?" Nasarov glanced up briefly at the interpreter when the question was asked, then nodded. *How much do they know, anyway?* he wondered.

"Do you admit to stealing merchandise earlier this evening?"

Nasarov shrugged and studied the upper right corner of the ceiling with some interest.

"If you hold Russian citizenship, the Russian Embassy can assist you."

"No," said the interpreter rapidly, as the previously sullen Nasarov began speaking loudly and angrily, gesticulating with both hands. "I do not want the Russian Embassy. I am not Russian. I am *Chechen. Ya nye hachu nikakoi pomoshchi ot Posolstva Russii!*"

"I am not Russian. I am Chechen," reported the interpreter. "I don't want any help from the Russian Embassy."

Liz noted irrelevantly that the suspect's nails were bitten down to the quick; some of the cuticles were bloody.

"They harass us, they kidnap and imprison us," sneered Nasarov as the interpreter continued his rapid interpretation. "Help from *them*? No, no Russian Embassy. *Nyet.* No Russians. *Posoltsva Nyet!*" He spat on the floor with contempt, then returned to silent mode, rubbing one hand atop the other.

"You do understand that you are being charged with a very serious offence?" asked Liz.

When the interpreter finished asking the question, Nasarov stared hard at Liz in a scornful and somehow menacing fashion. She took a quick breath.

Eyes still fixed on Liz, he replied, "*Da.*"

The interpreter said, "Yes."

"You will need to remain in custody until you go to court. Do you have any family here?"

"*Nyet.*"

"No," said the interpreter.

"Is there anyone you would like us to call?"

"*Nyet.*"

"No."

Liz and Ouellette looked at each other and back to the silent Nasarov. He looked up at Liz scornfully, then cast his eyes downward to his hands. He was slightly surprised to see them rubbing themselves.

After a moment, Ouellette asked, "What are you doing in Ottawa?"

The man darted a quick look at the sergeant then looked down at the green table.

He muttered something that sounded very like "business." The interpreter duly reported, "business."

"Oh yes?" pursued Liz. "What kind of business?"

"*Moi biznes,*" retorted the man angrily.

"My business," said the interpreter as Nasarov resumed his study of the table before him.

Liz glanced at Ouellette, then back at the man. *If there's a time to roll the dice*, she thought, *this is it*. She drew a short breath and waited for the man's dark eyes to meet hers.

Cultural Attaché Stanislav Ivanov placed the telephone slowly back into its cradle. The duty officer from the Russian Embassy had called to advise him that some Chechen had been picked up for shoplifting at a big Canadian department store—a historic chain and one that he frequented himself, reflected Ivanov. Good-quality clothing.

The man, who apparently spoke neither English nor French, was being held at the Elgin Street station. Ivanov knew where it was.

Damned Chechens, he thought. Causing enough trouble back in Russia and now creating havoc over here as well. The demonstrations, the murders, now some damned shoplifter.

He sat down, poured himself a short vodka, and lit a cigarette. He could go to the police station to see what was going on, although this was clearly a matter for the embassy's consular section. Whatever these Chechens believed, they were still Russian citizens. Of course Ivanov had a special brief to keep an eye on the Chechen community in Canada. And they had certainly been keeping him busy enough.

Especially the stunning widow Madina. He knew he shouldn't have started anything there, but really, how could he have resisted? His wife had left him years ago and a man had his needs. Anyway, part of his job was to keep apprised of developments in the Chechen community, and he was doing that, alright. Not that he had informed Moscow just how intimately he was following these developments.

The blue-eyed Chechen beauty had caught his eye immediately. It had been easy enough to find out where she lived, what her habits were, and then to stage a couple of casual encounters. Despite her demure nature and hatred of Russians in general, she had been flattered by the attentions of the handsome, charming diplomat and was relieved to have someone to speak with in a language she understood.

He'd never had a Chechen before. Of course he had told her they would marry.

Ivanov didn't know if Canadian security was on to him or not. He didn't really care. If they tried to blackmail him, he would just tell the ambassador and his handlers in Moscow that the affair was simply part of his effort to infiltrate the Chechen community in Canada. They had swallowed that sort of line before.

He tipped back the rest of the vodka, looking ruefully at the empty glass. He had been planning a quiet evening and was quickly concluding that this was, in fact, a consular matter. He could be briefed in the morning quickly enough. Ivanov picked up the phone and dialled the number of the embassy's consular chief.

"So, Bula Sergeyevich," inquired Liz politely, "I will ask you again, what brings you to Ottawa?"

The man calling himself Rasul Nasarov flinched.

Liz had explained her suspicions to Sergeant Ouellette earlier in the evening. Ouellette studied the man's reaction closely. The Chechen's face had turned even more ashen than before and perspiration was beading his upper lip.

"Rasul," said the man quietly and with a slight tremor. "*Menya zovut Rasul.*"

"Rasul. My name is Rasul," said the interpreter.

"No," said Liz, leaning back calmly in her chair and shaking her head. "I don't think so. I think that you are Bula Sergeyevich Gavrikov. The much-loved younger brother of Laila Daudova." She held his gaze although he desperately wanted to look away. "As you know, Laila was murdered in front of the Russian Embassy while attending a demonstration. She believed the Russians had made you disappear. She wanted nothing more than to find you."

"Russians," said the man, followed by an expletive that the interpreter hadn't heard before but guessed at "bastards."

"You haven't answered my question, Mr. Gavrikov," continued Liz. *Actually, he* had *answered it*, she reflected. He hadn't tried very hard to convince her that he was not, in fact, Laila Daudova's missing brother.

"Why didn't you come to Canada with Laila and Rasul? They waited for you until the last minute and then they had to leave. Where were you?"

Gavrikov glared at her. He was becoming angry. Who was this bitch to ask him where he was, what he was doing? *Some minor official in a tin-pot country*, he thought. *Some little whore in uniform.*

"No, I did not come with them to Canada," he said through the interpreter. "At one time I wanted to come to the West. I was young. Then . . . *then*," he snorted, "I learned what the West really is."

Liz tilted her head in inquiry and watched him steadily.

Gavrikov continued. "A sham. A lie. Countries united only in their hatred of Islam. Western elites preach democracy and freedom. But their actions are full of hate. They are hypocrites. *Murdering* hypocrites."

The Public Service interpreter was perspiring heavily now. It was difficult to simply interpret the language without reacting to the content of Bula's speech. The interpreter focused as much as he could on finding the right words, correcting the syntax and searching for logic in what the man was saying. But it was difficult to find logic where there seemed to be none. He plunged ahead nonetheless, trying to convey the content of the rant to the detectives.

"Laila and Rasul seemed to like it here," said Liz quietly, although her heart was racing. She struggled to keep her voice steady. "They were trying to make a new life for themselves."

"*Akh, da*," sneered Gavrikov in reply to the interpreter's statement.

"Oh, yes."

"So," said Liz softly, "how did you find out this *truth* about the West? Where?"

Gavrikov said nothing but narrowed his eyes in disgust.

"These people who taught you this *truth*—did they live in Chechnya? Or did you learn about the West in another place?"

Gavrikov maintained his silence.

"You see," said Liz. "I am very interested in the truth. I think it's extremely important. I would be interested to learn who taught you about this. For instance," she said, "I think you travelled out of Chechnya sometimes, didn't you?" After a brief pause, she added, "At least that's what Rasul told us."

"Rasul!" exclaimed the man, abruptly breaking his silence, then growling something beneath his breath.

"Yes, Rasul. Speaking of Rasul," Liz said, as though struck by a new idea, "tell me, can you think of anyone who might have wanted to kill your sister Laila and her husband?"

Gavrikov suddenly and unexpectedly switched to English. Heavily accented but very correct English. The interpreter, who had been trying to keep his emotions under control for some minutes, found his brain doing what it was so well trained to do and began interpreting Gavrikov's English into Russian before he realized what he was doing. He lapsed into silence, sweating heavily and wondering why the heat in this office had been set so high.

"The Russians, of course," said Gavrikov sourly. "Of course the Russians. Laila was in front of their embassy, demonstrating. Of course they would want her dead. And her husband."

"It must have been very painful for you to learn of their deaths," said Liz sympathetically. "I think you were already in Canada at the time, weren't you?" she asked.

"Painful," said Gavrikov slowly, as though learning an unknown word. He gave a short laugh. "Painful? Why is it painful for adulterers and infidels to die?"

Liz inhaled quickly and felt, rather than saw, Ouellette flinch.

Trying to keep her voice level, Liz asked, "Adulterers? They were legally married in Canada."

"In *Canada*!" He spat out the name of the country as though it were an epithet. "How long had they been together before they came to Canada? How long had they been here before they got married?

"My *dear* sister," he said viciously, "was a good Muslim girl. Then she starts thinking about going west. I know what Western women are," he said with an ugly smirk at Liz. "She already had Western ideas. Already *being*"—he spat out the word—"with Rasul." He shook his head in disgust.

"She abandoned her faith. Sure, she still called herself a Muslim, but her life was a blasphemy. Leaving home with a man not her husband? Laila was an infidel. A whore. They were both . . ." Here his English failed him, as he tried to find the equivalent word for a man and came up empty-handed. "Whores!" he said furiously.

Gavrikov was leaning across the table now. His clenched fists sat square on the table. A muscle was working hard in his jaw and dark blue veins stood out on his temples. Ouellette continued to take notes but was on high alert.

"They deserved to die," said Gavrikov angrily. "Laila disgraced our family. Thanks to God, there were no children."

The liaison officer and Ottawa police constable watched the interview nervously from the other side of the mirror, realizing they might have to intervene at any moment but awaiting a signal to act.

"So," said Liz. "You came to this country bent on killing your sister and her husband because you thought they were adulterers."

Gavrikov shook his head.

"Actually," she said, "we know that you did this."

Gavrikov turned a lighter shade of grey but said nothing.

"Wouldn't you like to know *how* we know?"

Ouellette, writing quickly, was very curious to know how Liz knew that this man had killed the Daudovs. Or was she trying something out?

Meanwhile, Gavrikov glared defiantly at Liz.

"Well," she said quietly, leaning across the desk, "we found the AK-47 in your apartment earlier this evening. Doubtless it has your fingerprints all over it. And Ballistics is comparing it with the bullets found in both Laila and Rasul. You know they will match."

Ouellette knew they had done no such thing and was tempted to grin at the audacity of his boss, but kept his head down and continued writing.

Finally Gavrikov erupted. "Oh yes," he cried. "Clever, clever bitch! Yes, I killed them both. And I feel good," he said, nodding his head and squaring his shoulders. "Very, very good. I did what was right in the eyes of God."

Liz nodded slowly, trying not to manifest the relief she felt. In her experience, gambles like this rarely paid off, but she hadn't had a lot of choice.

"What I want to know, though," she said, "is if you acted alone."

Gavrikov, thinking of his friend or, well, his handler in Etobicoke, shook his head. He knew that the group that claimed his loyalty had plans, big plans, and he was not about to give away anything that would jeopardize the jihad. "No," he said, "it was just me." And he stuck to that story for the rest of the interview.

They left the interview room with Gavrikov, sullen but placid enough, in handcuffs. The liaison officer, interpreter, and Ottawa police constable followed in silence, the constable carrying Gavrikov's black, puffy ski jacket.

Suddenly a fair-haired man in a well-tailored suit stood up from a chair close to the entrance of the station. The duty constable didn't have time for formalities, as the young man announced, "I am Artur Zhakarov, First Secretary of the Consular Department at the Russian Embassy. I am here to offer any assistance . . ." He got no further, as Gavrikov spat for the third time that evening but not, this time, at the floor.

As Liz and Ouellette drove through the silent streets, Ouellette said, "So it was, as you suspected, a so-called honour killing?"

"I wanted to be wrong."

"What madness is that?" muttered Ouellette, steering carefully around an icy corner. "His own sister?" He suddenly felt a desire to call his own sister, Josée, in Trois Rivières. "Do you think he's crazy?"

Liz looked over at her sergeant. "I don't know," she said. "It can be hard to tell with zealots. Not our call."

"But what started you thinking it might be Bula?" The squad car skidded slightly to the left.

"Simply because he was, well, the only piece of the puzzle who wasn't there, if you see what I mean."

The sergeant had to concentrate on his driving but said, no, he wasn't sure he knew what she meant.

"Well, he was central to the story. The whole case revolved around the disappearance of Bula Gavrikov. And he was the only one I couldn't account for. So when you dug up that information at Immigration on the three refugee claimants, it started to come together—in my mind, at least. Of course there was no proof. When I saw him tonight, I was sure that I had seen him before. It was in the picture that Laila was carrying during the demonstration, before she was killed. He looks a lot older now, though."

Ouellette nodded and turned the heater down a notch. "What about the other refugee claimants?" he asked.

"I don't know. In fact, let's find out what the OPP found out about the other two claimants in Ontario. I wouldn't be surprised if there was some connection with at least one of them."

Liz noticed Ouellette taking a surreptitious glance at his watch. It was late and the adrenalin had long since evaporated.

"Not tonight, Sergeant. It'll keep. Anyway, the OPP has them both under surveillance."

Ouellette smiled wryly and nodded. It was already past one o'clock.

SIXTEEN
Canada

During the meeting of the task force, which took place the following afternoon, Liz's superintendent looked as proud as if he had, personally and without assistance, delivered twins. His ruddy face was glowing and he was puffed up to a greater extent than usual as he congratulated Liz, Ouellette, and the other members of the team for a job well done.

Liz briefed the team on the previous evening's activities. Gavrikov was currently being held by Ottawa police while further inquiries were made, but she had no doubt that they had their man; he had said as much. But a case had to be built for the courts, and the police would be busy for some time.

When Gavrikov's motel room had been searched early that morning, an AK-47 was in fact found, as Liz had suspected. It had been dusted for fingerprints, and one set matched Gavrikov's. This seemed sloppy to Liz, but she guessed that the Chechen had used gloves for the crimes, but hadn't thought to do so if he was moving the gun around in the room. There were also a couple of partial prints on them, which had not yet been identified. Other personal belongings amounted to nothing more than a couple of T-shirts, one of them with the name of an American football team emblazoned on it, some underwear, and a small, battered suitcase.

"Sometimes," Liz said to the team, "weapons are smuggled in pieces and assembled here. Or the rifle might have been purchased here in Canada. We haven't come up with any leads on that yet, but we'll have to continue investigating."

"So," asked a young constable, "is he just a nutter, or had he become radicalized or something?"

"I'm not sure. Maybe a bit of both. This radicalization business isn't a subject I know a lot about. Perhaps CSIS has a better line on this," she said, shooting a quick look at Fletcher, but the CSIS man remained silent.

"It's a new area to me," Liz continued, "but clearly Gavrikov somehow turned from a loving little brother into some sort of extremist. Daudov told us that Gavrikov 'liked to travel,'" she said, making quotation mark signs in the air. "Maybe on his travels he met some radical types who were interested in recruiting naïve young men. Or women, I guess," she added doubtfully.

"Anyway, all that I know is that some Islamic radicalization is taking place in South Asia, in parts of Afghanistan, and in Pakistan. I believe sometimes it takes place farther to the north in some of the new states created after the fall of the Soviet Union—and maybe parts of the Middle East. I'm quite out of my depth here." She paused and again looked at Fletcher to see if he had anything to add, but he was busy taking notes.

Sighing inwardly, she went on. "Whatever 'training' or brainwashing took place, Gavrikov ended up with excellent weapons skills and a fierce hatred of the West and anything that resembled it. Including the so-called adulterous relationship between Daudov and Gavrikov's older sister, Laila."

Ouellette entered the room, looking tired but excited.

"Gilles?" enquired Liz.

"I just got off the phone with the OPP. They've had this other refugee chap, Limonov, of Etobicoke, on their radar for a while. He'd been under surveillance because the OPP has connected him to some sort of funny business concerning weapons. He seems to have quickly become the 'go-to' guy for firearms, according to some gang plants in the Toronto area. A lot of disreputable people were coming and going from his place at all hours." He consulted his notes. "Yeah," he continued, "weapons supply, assembly, upgrades, that sort of thing."

"Like maybe putting together a disassembled AK-47?" asked Liz, trying to hide her excitement.

"Well, yeah, I suppose so," said Gilles, raising his

eyebrows. "Anyhow," he continued, "When I told the OPP we wanted to talk to this guy, they told me he'd already been brought in on weapons charges.

"From what the OPP said, this Limonov comes across as quite irrational—much like our Gavrikov. In any event, they've made the link between the two men; Limonov has said that he knows Gavrikov, although he may well be trying to make Gavrikov the fall guy for everything, including the weapons charges. But they seem to have enough on him to make the charges stick to him like glue."

"So," said Liz, thinking aloud, "we don't yet know exactly what their association was and to what extent they were aware of one another's activities. We'll follow up with Limonov later in the day. We need to know their movements and when and where they met up. Have you told the OPP we'll be down?"

"Yes," replied Ouellette. "I told them they can expect us this afternoon."

Liz nodded. "Meanwhile, I think we can be pretty sure that Limonov was the guy who furnished Gavrikov with the weapon that killed both Laila and Rasul Daudov. In fact, I'll bet the partial set of prints on the gun are from Limonov. With any luck we can wrap up a lot of those details today.

"But I wouldn't be surprised if their connection goes a lot deeper than that. Limonov might even have been Gavrikov's 'handler,' or at least a resource for Gavrikov as he carried out his plans.

"Actually," she said, switching gears, "the AK-47 is a very reliable weapon but not usually terribly accurate. I was always a bit surprised that it would be the weapon of choice for what were, essentially, two sniper-style attacks. Maybe this Limonov was able to improve the accuracy of the weapon destined for Gavrikov. In fact," she mused, "I wouldn't be surprised if we didn't come across more of these rifles in future. There are a lot of them floating around since the collapse of the Soviet Union."

"Private enterprise," interposed Ouellette.

"Exactly," said Liz with a grim smile.

Greg Gibson had been listening to the discussion with great attention, drumming the fingers of his right hand rapidly on the table before him. He asked, "There was a third refugee, wasn't there, who arrived about the same time as Gavrikov and entered at Pearson? Does it look like he was involved as well?"

Ouellette shook his head. "No, this . . ." he consulted a piece of paper, ". . . Volodin . . . didn't appear to have anything to do with anything and had documented his movements in great detail in hopes of having his refugee claim accepted. His movements and contacts check out. Poor guy was apparently terrified the police thought he was involved in the murders and that he'd be deported. But so far it looks as though he's in the clear."

"Gavrikov didn't have much of an exit strategy, did he?" asked Gibson.

"No," agreed Liz. "He may have thought he wouldn't get away with the murders in the first place. Or he was just so blinkered by his conviction that his so-called family honour had been tarnished that he didn't really think through what would happen afterwards."

Her thoughts took another turn and she suggested,

"Possibly 'Limonov of Etobicoke' was supposed to help him get out of the country, until Gavrikov made the stupid mistake of shoplifting."

"Although you were already staking out his motel," added the Super, beaming ever more broadly.

Liz smiled back. "It was worth a try. And it could conceivably have paid off for him if he'd learned we were on to him, except that he decided to celebrate with some shoplifted caviar."

"I wonder if the family even cared about the 'honour' thing," mused Ouellette. "We have no way of knowing, at least yet, if the family even knew about—let alone condoned—Gavrikov's sick plan. They may just have been happy that their daughter had managed to escape a war zone and start a new life with a man she loved."

"So, then," said a young female officer, hoping that she wasn't asking a stupid question, "these three men came in as refugees. Do we know if that's how the others in the Chechen community came in?"

Liz regarded the eager young officer. She reminded Liz, just a little, of her own, younger self.

"Some of them were legitimate refugees," Liz nodded. "Although there is no official record of some of the others— including Rasul and Laila Daudov—entering the country. There seems to be some sort of people-smuggling organization operating in Central Asia and moving these people to North America and Western Europe—at a very stiff price, no doubt.

"There also seems to be a roaring trade in high-quality fake documentation, including Canadian passports and visas. We don't know how large the operation is or where it's headquartered, and it will be difficult to get much information from those who came to the country via that route. This is out of our hands, anyway, so it's not anything that we'll be involved with investigating."

"Why not?" the young officer asked, chagrined.

"That part of the investigation will start with our Immigration and Passport Branch."

Ouellette sighed. He knew that particular branch of the RCMP was small and underfunded, staffed by a small group of solid, seasoned veterans, all of whom looked as though they hadn't slept in weeks.

Liz said, "They probably already have some notion of where fake documents are being produced and they will be in touch with the relevant embassy's liaison officer. The investigation will start from there and will probably involve everyone from the local authorities to the Passport Office at External Affairs, Immigration and, of course, our good friends at CSIS. It will doubtless be pretty messy in terms of jurisdiction." She shot Fletcher a wry smile, which was not returned as Fletcher had his head down and was rapidly taking notes with one hand and scratching his nose with the other.

Ouellette was also looking at Fletcher. While Ouellette had joined the RCMP some years after the creation of CSIS, he was acutely aware of the continuing lack of trust between the two agencies. CSIS had been created in 1981, as a reaction to RCMP "dirty tricks" in the fraught aftermath of the national crisis involving the so-called Front de la libération du Québec. Ouellette always cringed a little, internally, when reminded of the FLQ. Although he had only been a boy in 1970, during what became known as the "October Crisis," he was aware that his black sheep uncle on his mother's side, Daniel, had been an FLQ sympathizer at the time.

Many in the RCMP still regarded CSIS with suspicion and considered its agents to be bogus police officers believing themselves a cut above their opposite numbers in the RCMP. Most annoying was CSIS's ongoing refusal to share information with other agencies and its tireless invocation of the convenient excuse, "need to know."

Ouellette was roused from his ruminations about the spooks in CSIS when he heard a female constable ask, "So what was the role of Independence United in this? Anything?"

Liz was happy to open the floor to Ouellette, and he was more than happy to tell his colleagues exactly what he thought of that small group of activists.

SEVENTEEN
Canada

Liz was immensely relieved that the murders of Laila Daudova and Rasul Daudov had been solved. She'd finally had a good night's sleep and was starting to feel like a real human being again. Major crimes, especially homicides, became all-consuming for her, relegating everything else in life to second place. Except, perhaps, Rochester. And, to Liz's surprise, Detective Chief Inspector Stephen Hay. She had wondered on several occasions during the investigation how he might approach certain things; she admired his detached, intensely methodical approach to his work. She doubted that he would ever rely on "hunches" or gut feelings. Rather,

Hay tended to take a big-picture view of a crime. At the same time, no detail was too small to notice. At least this was the impression she had developed of him during their work together in London.

She wanted to see him again. She had enjoyed talking to him and missed his comfortable presence. Liz hadn't thought along these lines for a very long time. She wondered if this might finally be something special.

At present, she was taking a long walk through the dim, frozen streets of Aylmer with Rochester trotting along happily and sniffing delightedly at anything that looked remotely disgusting.

Liz finally concluded that she should do something about it. She decided to call Hay and make a concrete suggestion that they meet somewhere for a few days, even though the idea was alien and deeply unnerving. She had never in her life asked anyone for a date, let alone to go on a holiday. Enough men had been interested in her—at least until they learned of her profession—for her never to have wanted for male companionship.

She found first dates more trouble than they were worth anyway and didn't seek out potential companions, let alone partners. On Saturday nights, her preference was to curl up on the couch and watch an old black-and-white movie on TVO. If her line of work didn't deter her from wanting a permanent relationship, her previous marriage to a controlling and manipulative charmer did. Loads of personality and no character; she never wanted to go through that again.

In spite of the views befitting a woman of her generation

and profession, Liz still privately wished that Hay would make the first move. True, he had called a couple of times, and there had been that uncomfortable suggestion of them getting together at an Interpol conference (*an Interpol conference, for crying out loud*) but she concluded that if she left it up to him she might be waiting for a very long time.

She looked at her watch. London was five hours ahead. It was now 3:23 in Aylmer. She took a big gulp of cold air and said, "No time like the present, eh boy?"

Rochester wagged his agreement. They made their way back to the house, although Liz was walking more slowly than usual. She was still unsure whether her decision was the right one.

Liz kicked off her boots, wiped Rochester's feet, changed into her sweats, poured herself a glass of wine, and lit a smoke.

She sat down on her couch and dialled Hay's number. She heard a series of beeps on the other end and finally his phone began to ring. By the fourth ring, she was getting ready to hang up in some relief when suddenly he answered.

"Hay."

"Forsyth."

"Hello," he said, genuinely pleased. "Just came through the door. Bit of a long day. How are you?"

Liz heard some scuffling on the end of the line, which sounded as if Hay was kicking his shoes off.

"I'm fine, actually. Really happy to have got to the bottom of the Daudov murders."

"Yes, congratulations. It's been in the papers and the

Yard's morning briefing. I was, in fact, intending to call you, but you beat me to it. I'm never sure when you'll be home."

Liz laughed. "I have the same problem. How are things going at your end? The press here hasn't been reporting on the Bouchard murder for a few days now—found other crimes or scandals, no doubt."

"That damned case is going nowhere in a hurry. And working its way down the pile. We started off with nothing but an ID, and we don't have a lot more now. It's bloody frustrating, but there's not a whole lot more to follow up on. Sometimes I wish I were one of the television cops."

"I've thought that, too. How are you keeping otherwise? And Wilkins?"

"Quite well, really, thanks. Wilkins is fine. Still dating the lovely Gemma. Probably get married one of these days."

"How long have they been going out?" she asked.

"No idea. She seems to have always been around."

At this there was a short silence, broken by Hay's inquiry into Rochester's health. Rochester seemed to understand that he was the subject of conversation, as he grinned and rolled over onto his back, a soggy rawhide bone still in his mouth.

After more small talk—if one considers murder small talk—Liz finally took a deep breath and was about to broach the actual subject of her call when Hay broke in to say, "Look, Liz, I've been thinking. I'd really like to see you again. I very much enjoyed your company last month, despite the circumstances of course." He had run out of the deep breath that *he* had taken, and flopped back into his wingchair to let fate take its course.

Liz exhaled and said, "I've been thinking along the same lines."

"You have? Glad to hear it. Do you have any ideas?"

"Well, actually, yes," said Liz, deciding she might as well come clean. "Maybe we could meet up in France for a couple of days or something. I have scads of overtime and we're on a use-it-or-lose-it sort of scheme." As soon as she said that, she felt her colour rising and was very glad that they were only on the phone.

"That sounds lovely. You really wouldn't mind coming all the way out here just for a few days?"

"It's not really all that far. And there are direct flights daily from Montreal and Toronto," she said. "At least that's what I've been told," she added quickly.

"Yes, wonderful," said Hay. "What sort of time frame were you thinking?"

"I'm pretty flexible at the moment, and nobody will miss me for a few days." Rochester looked at her briefly and whined, then resumed chewing on his bone. "Your schedule sounds pretty packed, though."

"Nothing that's going anywhere. What do you think about early February? Would that work for you?"

"Yes, yes it would. Shall I start looking at flights?"

"Yes, do. That would be brilliant. And I can start looking into hotels and what not . . ." Now he was changing colour a little.

With this more or less sorted, they rang off.

EIGHTEEN
England

Susan Beck of Penicuik, Scotland, joined the rowdy group at the bar next door to the Willkommen Hostel. It was about six, and she was hungry. Her companions were an interesting mixture of Americans, Germans, Australians, and French. They were all roughly the same age and split pretty evenly along gender lines. Some had been staying at the hostel for a couple of months; some, like Susan, had only been there a week or two. Apparently, years ago, a tradition had been established that the residents of the hostel would meet up around six for a drink and a bite to eat. The tradition had somehow stuck despite the hundreds of changes in clientele.

The next-door bar was old but not historic, run-down but not charming, dim but lacking in ambience. It was, however, clean and inexpensive, and while the food was pedestrian, it was filling. So the Drop Inn did quite a good trade from the young tourists from the hostel. The young people didn't cause a lot of trouble, apart from the odd problem due to an excess of drink and testosterone. Nothing untoward had happened lately, though. The worst the staff had had to put up with was the noise and laughter of the travellers as they recounted their latest adventures.

Susan felt comfortable here. The people were friendly and happy, and they seemed to welcome her as an old friend. The benches in the booths were wide and comfortable, and she didn't have to squeeze onto some skinny wooden chair. Susan kept to herself, always a bit shy in company, but she enjoyed watching the others and hearing their stories.

She ordered a Coke and spaghetti Bolognese. She looked at a few posters on the wall that she hadn't noticed before—mostly ads for long-forgotten concerts or advertisements for money-lending operations.

"Mind if I join you?"

Susan started, then looked up into the face of the young man who'd helped her get back to the hostel the other day.

"Of course," she said, then faltered, "I mean, no, I don't mind at all."

He ordered a pint and asked Susan how her visit was going so far. She told him what she had done in the last few days, including a coach trip to Hampton Court. As she looked at him in the dim light, she realized he wasn't as unattractive as she had thought at first.

At his home in Pimlico, DCI Hay was looking into the cost of hotels in Paris during early February. This was a pleasant enough task, although he was beginning to realize that he and Forsyth had left much unsaid during their telephone conversation, and that he had a number of decisions to make. *One room or two? Two, definitely two. Mustn't be presumptuous.*

He took a swig of coffee and listened to the rain sluicing down outside. Would they each be paying for their own room? Yes, no doubt Forsyth would insist. What sort of price range? This was tricky. He didn't want them to go to a dump, but prices were high in Paris, even in February, and he had no idea what her financial situation was.

He lit a cigarette and took a long drag. What part of Paris? No idea. For how long? She had said "a few days" but he wasn't sure exactly what that meant. In fact, they had decided virtually nothing during their phone call the previous day.

Hay decided to propose a series of options. Scenarios, hypotheses, the sort of thing the police were expected to come up with. Three hotels, ranging in price and location. Must also check out what was going on at museums and theatres and such. Or did she go in for that sort of thing? Hay was beginning to realize that he didn't really know much about Liz Forsyth at all. Not a clue, really. But he did want to find out. Could come up with a few more scenarios concerning things she might want to do.

He took another drag from his cigarette, reviewing the notes he had been scribbling about the trip. Suddenly the phone rang, interrupting his pleasant, if somewhat confused, thoughts about the proposed holiday.

Superintendent Neilson sounded tense, and his voice was about an octave higher than usual.

"We have another one," he said. "Young woman, long hair, naked, large. In a small park in Battersea. I want you there immediately."

Hay took down the details and hung up the phone. He squashed out his cigarette and mechanically put on his raincoat and boots. *Another one*, he thought. *Surely not.* But it sounded sickeningly similar. He locked the door behind him. This was not going to be a good day. Another murder—maybe one of Wilkins's "cereal killers"? He realized unhappily that he wouldn't be able to go away any time soon. *And now*, he thought, *I'll have to tell Forsyth.*

ACKNOWLEDGMENTS

I am extremely grateful to many people for their support and enthusiasm for this book, starting with Taryn Boyd and her team at Touchwood Editions in Victoria. As always, TouchWood's professionalism and commitment, combined with its interactive approach, make it a pleasure to work with. My editor, Frances Thorsen, again contributed her experience and insight in shaping the book, for which I am most appreciative.

For providing both expert advice and solid friendship, many thanks to RCMP Chief Superintendent Lynn Twardosky (ret'd) and RCMP Superintendent MSM Claude Theriault (ret'd). Thanks as well to Eric Hussey, (ret'd) of the Metropolitan Police, London for providing invaluable local context and specifics. I must also extend my deep appreciation to BC coroner Barbara McLintock for taking the time to discuss over lunch things not normally considered suitable at lunch!

The steadfast support, along with sales and signing opportunities, provided by Sidney Pharmasave went far beyond what could be expected from any local business, and I am extremely grateful for the friendship and encouragement that the great people at Pharmasave have provided me from the beginning of my writing endeavours.

My thanks go out to my dearest friend of more decades than either of us want to admit, Alison Green, for her staunch friendship, unwavering support, and oft-needed pep talks.

I also want to thank my brother Cliff and his wife Julie for their ongoing enthusiasm and encouragement.

For Ian Hill, I am very grateful, not only for his enduring support and constancy, but also for holding my feet to the fire whenever I've wanted to take the easy way out.

To all my other dear friends and neighbours who have shared my excitement in this adventure, thank you all so much. In particular I would like to mention Ann Cronin-Cossette, Christine Rollo, Lee Emerson, and Frank Haigh.

And to my sister-in-law Chantal, to whom this book is dedicated, my sincere thanks for always being there.